She did the s...

She reached up an... along his jawline, j... bristly, so many hou... morning shave. And... she stood on her tiptoes and kissed him. Lightly, just a friendly little goodbye-between-friends peck on the mouth.

Which didn't end right away. No, there were sensations to record first: the surprising softness of his mouth, the firm, smooth skin of his lips. She held back... but still, she lingered, just for a moment or two. She'd kissed him before, of course, but as an afterthought. This was no longer an afterthought.

Available in June 2008 from Mills & Boon® Intrigue

One Hot Target
DIANE PERSHING

MILLS & BOON
Pure reading pleasure

*All the characters in this book have no existence outside the
imagination of the author, and have no relation whatsoever to anyone
bearing the same name or names. They are not even distantly inspired
by any individual known or unknown to the author, and all the
incidents are pure invention.*

*First published in Great Britain 2008
by Harlequin Mills & Boon Limited,
Eton House, 18-24 Paradise Road, Richmond, Surrey TW9 1SR*

© Diane Pershing 2007

ISBN: 978 0 263 85970 6

46-0608

*Harlequin Mills & Boon policy is to use papers that are
natural, renewable and recyclable products and made from
wood grown in sustainable forests. The logging and
manufacturing processes conform to the legal environmental
regulations of the country of origin.*

*Printed and bound in Spain
by Litografia Rosés S.A., Barcelona*

DIANE PERSHING

For more years than she cares to disclose, Diane Pershing made her living as an actress and singer. She was extremely contented in these professions, except for one problem – there was way too much downtime, and she worried that her brain was atrophying. So she took up pen and paper and began writing, first for television, then as a movie critic, then as a novelist.

She wrote her first novel, *Sultry Whispers,* following the dictum to "write what you know," and it was about a voiceover actress who battled the male-dominated mind-set of advertising agencies. There have been fifteen more sales since. Diane is happy to report that there is no more downtime in her life; indeed, with writing and acting – and teaching classes in both – she now faces the dilemma of not having enough time, which she says is a quality problem indeed. She loves to hear from readers, so please write to her at PO Box 67424, Los Angeles, CA 90067, USA or online at diane@dianepershing.com. You can also visit Diane's website at www.dianepershing. com.

Dear Reader,

I'm not sure why I've always been attracted to flaky people. You know, the type who lose things, are always running late and sincerely apologetic about it. Maybe it's because I'm pretty responsible myself and kind of yearn sometimes *not* to be, even though – yes, yes, I know – being responsible makes me a better member of society, etc.

I've written one of those flaky folks in *One Hot Target,* and I had the very best time doing it! Carmen is lovable, good-natured, enthusiastic and emotional…and just can't seem to get her life together. Because she's based on a couple of friends of mine, she just flowed out of my brain and onto the computer, as though channelled.

During the course of the novel she changes somewhat, out of necessity. It seems her life is *seriously* in danger and action must be taken so she can continue to breathe the air on this planet. But she also needs to change so that she and her best friend (who's been in love with her forever) – the decidedly male, emphatically logical, most definitely *not* flaky JR – will have a chance of any kind of life together. Oh, and JR needs to do some changing himself; after all, it takes two to make unrequited love into the requited kind, right?

Enjoy. I think you will.

Love,

Diane

Chapter 1

"I can't believe it, JR. Me, here at Nordstrom, in the workplace department, in a *suit*. A *business* suit!"

As she ranted into her cell phone, Carmen stared at the dressing-room mirror's reflection with intense displeasure. She stuck her tongue out at the image, then spoke again into the mouthpiece. "I mean, you know me, JR, the original antifashion thrift-shop junkie. I've been a retro hippie, a recovering Goth—" she pivoted to get a view of the rear and made another disgruntled face "—but I've never, *ever,* been someone who even looked at a straight, desk-sitting, member-of-the-office-staff-and-proud-of-it *suit!*"

On the other end of the line, JR, who had, poor thing, heard Carmen's tirades before, said mildly, "How does it look?"

She frowned again, then shrugged. "I don't know. I

mean, I have no frame of reference. How is a suit supposed to look?"

"Well, does it fit?"

"I guess. The saleslady said this was my size and it isn't too tight or too loose, so yeah, I guess it fits. But it's *gray,* JR," she griped to her very best friend in all the world. "With these little *pinstripes.* And the saleslady gave me this lavender blouse. A *blouse.* I mean, really. With *buttons.*"

"Oh, no," JR said with mock horror. "Not buttons."

"And I'm going to have to wear *hose.* I never wear hose. *Ever.*"

"Hey, kid, welcome to the world of grown-ups."

"Yeah, I know." Carmen sighed loudly, then made yet one more face at the mirror. "It's time. I get it. But I don't have to like it."

And she didn't like it, not at all.

Goldie Raquel Coyle, known as "Carmen" since age seven when she'd been introduced to Bizet's opera and had fallen in love with the tragic heroine—to the point of insisting on a Spanish lady-of-the-night costume for Halloween that year—had made every attempt in the world to not grow up. But she was one year shy of thirty, and it was, alas, finally time.

She had to get a job. A real job. Not a clerk at a used records store, nor a fast-food takeout counter person. Most definitely not a house-sitter/dog-walker/part-time errands runner. Those were items on her old résumé, and would no longer do. She needed money, real money. She had bills to pay.

Well, they weren't really her bills, but Tio's. The jerk. They'd lived together in her little house for three months and she'd had no idea he'd been dealing. None. He'd run up all kinds of debt on her credit card, borrowed money in her name from her friends. Never even paid his half of the rent and had spent her half. And she hadn't known. Not any of it. Not until he'd taken off, never to be heard from again. And the phone calls had begun, followed by the pounding on the door, and it had all been a nightmare. Big-time stress situation. Carmen hated stress, hated hassles. Avoided them like the plague. Which meant—and she'd be the first to admit it—that she'd lived her particular time on earth too often under the radar, too often letting others clean up her mess after her.

Not anymore. She'd borrowed money from her family to cover Tio's debts and she would pay them back as quickly as possible. And this was the very last time she'd fall for another bad-boy type who was not what he claimed to be. She'd learned her lesson. About time.

"Carmen?" JR's voice in her earpiece pulled her out of her reverie.

"Does it have to be gray, JR? Couldn't it be…I don't know…yellow? A little sunshine to take away the gloom?"

She stared at the mirror. She'd already kicked off her sandals—fun, strappy things in bronze-, silver- and gold-dyed leather with a chartreuse rose on top that she'd picked up at the Nordstrom shoe sale not five minutes before coming up here—and was now on tippy-toes, trying to imagine herself in heels.

"Carmen," JR said, "I have a client coming in two minutes, so I have to get off the phone."

"Fine, desert me. I don't blame you. I look so drab. So boring."

"Not possible."

"Possible, trust me. I—"

Pop!

The noise, a soft, explosive sound, like a special effect on a computer game, was followed by a yelp of surprised pain.

Carmen stood still, unsure of what she had just heard, aware only that it felt off—wrong, somehow—and that it came from somewhere nearby.

Pop! Pop!

Two more of the same soft noises were followed by a strange smell—something burning? And something wet had just hit her lower leg. She glanced down and saw a spattering of red on her ankles and bare feet. The fitting-room walls were open at the bottom; the red spatters had come from the room to her left.

Blood. It was blood.

"Oh, my God."

"Carmen?" JR's voice was sharp. "What is it? What's wrong?"

A woman's groan came from next door, followed by the soft thud of running footsteps in the dressing-room corridor. "Someone's hurt," she whispered into the phone.

"Who? What are you talking about?"

"In the dressing room next door to me." She reached for the door handle. "I think she's been shot."

JR drew in a quick, alarmed breath. "Stay where you are. Do you hear me? Can you lock the door?"

Too late. Carmen had already opened the door to the dressing room a tiny crack and now peered down the long corridor that led to the selling floor. A figure was just disappearing around the corner, but not before she had enough time to register a fleeting impression of a slender form dressed head-to-toe in black. Running shoes, sweatpants, sweatshirt, a black baseball cap, no hair visible.

Another groan of pain made Carmen open her door wide and step out into the corridor.

"Carmen?" she heard JR say.

"I have to see how badly she's hurt," she whispered into the phone.

"Don't you dare! Stay just where you are. I'm calling 911."

"Do that…"

The slatted dressing-room door had a vertical line of three holes punched in it. She jiggled the knob, but the door was locked, so she peered through one of the holes.

A young woman lay slumped at an awkward angle, her upper body leaning against the mirror, the lower part on the floor, legs splayed. She wore a bra and panties; in her hand she clutched a navy dress with a small yellow-and-pink flower pattern, its tag hanging from the sleeve, as though she'd been about to try it on. Blood poured from her head and midsection onto the carpeted floor. The mirror was spattered with the red liquid.

Carmen felt bile rising in her throat, but she swallowed hard and ordered herself not to vomit. "JR," she said into her phone. "It's bad. Get an ambulance. I have to go."

Snapping the phone shut, she yelled, "Someone! Help!" as loudly as she could. Two dressing-room doors opened farther down the corridor, and two scared faces peeked out from them. "Get a doctor! Quickly," she told them.

Without waiting to see what they did, she lay flat on

her stomach and crawled under the door and into the small room.

Carmen had never seen a dying person before, but clearly this woman belonged in that category. Her breathing was labored and rattled harshly in her throat, her eyelids were half-open, only the whites visible. And blood pumped out of her midsection with a horrendously rapid, yet even, rhythm.

"Hold on," Carmen said, swallowing again to keep the contents of her stomach from coming up. "Help is coming."

The bleeding. She had to stop the bleeding. She got onto her knees and grabbed the flower-patterned dress, rolled it up into a ball and held it over the worst of the wounds, the jagged hole in the woman's stomach. In an instant, the dress was soaked.

"Hold on," she said again desperately, this time pulling off the suit jacket she was wearing and pushing it against the blood-soaked dress. She felt so powerless, so helpless to stop the inevitable. "Please," she said, aware that she was crying, "please hold on."

There was the sound of running feet again in the hallway, this time coming in her direction. "We're in here!" she called out. Someone tried the handle, but before Carmen could get up to unlock it, that same someone rammed against the slatted door, once, twice, three times. The door burst open. Carmen looked up to see a stocky, gray-haired woman standing over her.

"I'm a doctor," she said grimly. "Get back."

On her knees, Carmen scrambled away from the body, then stood and backed into the corridor, unable to take her eyes off the gunshot victim as the doctor worked on her. The breaths became louder and harsher, as did the awful rattling sounds emanating from her throat. This went on for several moments more until, at last, there was a loud, long sigh, and the woman was still.

The doctor attempted resuscitation for a few moments more, but to no avail. She shook her head then stood, checking her watch.

It was over. A life had ended.

Others were gathered in the corridor now, an excited buzz of curiosity filling the air. Someone, a manager-type, was saying, "Please, stand back. The ambulance is on its way and we need to make room."

Carmen took it all in, suddenly dissociated, feeling as though she were seeing details through the wrong end of a telescope. Her gaze remained focused on the poor young woman's lifeless body. Just moments ago, she'd been trying on clothing in the privacy of a well-appointed fitting room, just as Carmen had been doing next door. It had all happened so quickly. Why had she been shot? Who was she? Did she have a family? Children? Who would break the news to them? Would someone mourn her?

As her own breathing became labored she felt a scream rising in her throat. She clamped a hand over her mouth and, again, with a severe effort of will, tamped it down. This was *not* about her, she told herself. She was alive. But she couldn't stop the tears, nor the quaking sensation that seemed to affect every inch of her body. Sinking to the floor, she wrapped her arms around herself and rocked back and forth, fixated on death's latest statistic.

The strangest thing happened next. Earlier, she'd

taken in the woman's awkward position on the floor, the bra, the panties, the flowered dress, but now Carmen's gaze landed on her feet. As her addled brain registered a bizarre coincidence, she gasped out loud: she and the dead woman must have both recently shopped at the famous, twice-yearly Nordstrom shoe sale, and, obviously, the two of them must have shared the same taste. She knew this because on the victim's feet were the very same multicolored sandals that Carmen had bought not a half hour ago. The perky chartreuse rose on top was now stained brownish-red.

Her gaze fell on her own bent knees and she recoiled. She, too, was covered in blood—bare feet, legs, skirt, blouse. Even her hands. She stared at them, horrified. It was too much, way too much. Shivering, she leaned her head back against the wall and closed her eyes. This was a nightmare.

But at least you're alive, a little inner voice reminded her. The woman lying on the dressing-room floor could have been her, Carmen thought, and hated herself for the small surge of gratitude she felt that tragedy had struck someone else and not her. And then she stopped thinking at all.

In the thirty minutes since Carmen had so abruptly ended their phone call, JR observed, the scene had become bedlam. On the second floor of the mall, yellow crime-scene tape was stretched across the wide opening to the store. Crowds were gathered but being held back by private security and uniformed policemen. Outside, the whirring of overhead helicopters could be heard; inside, reporters and photographers were trying for a peek, a story, an angle.

JR fought his determined way through the crowd and reached one of the uniformed cops. "Excuse me," he said, "I have to get in there."

The young, clean-shaven face was impassive. "Sorry, no one allowed. This is a crime scene."

"I'm a lawyer and friend of the woman who found the body. She needs me."

"I don't care if you're the king of Spain, sir, no one is allowed in."

Just then he spotted Carmen on the other side of the tape, walking with that unconscious sensuality of hers, alongside a tall, middle-aged, brown-skinned man dressed in a worn-looking suit and whom JR assumed was a plainclothes cop. Carmen's arms were crossed and held close to her body, as though she were cold. Her hair was messy, her face was tear-stained and she wore faded jeans, rubber thong sandals and one of her droopy yet sexy peasant blouses. A shopping bag dangled from one arm, a large, bulky purse from the other.

"Carmen!" JR called out.

The cop glanced over, annoyance on his face. At the same time, Carmen looked up and saw him. "JR!" she called out and came running over to the edge of the yellow police tape, the man accompanying her following right behind. "You came!"

She threw her arms around his neck and he embraced her, held her close. And not for the first, or even the fiftieth, time, JR felt that sad, *hopeless* feeling at this intimate act of his body joined to hers. For Carmen, the act of hugging meant comfort, warmth, affection. For him, it meant all that, and a hell of a lot more. He cursed himself silently. Had he no spine at all? Hadn't he, just a couple of days ago, decided it had to end, that Carmen would not have this kind of effect on or power over him ever again?

Yeah, right. Tell it to his body, to his hormones.

To his soul.

He stroked her hair. "Poor baby. Are you okay?"

"Oh, JR." Her head was buried in his neck; he could feel moisture from her tears on the skin above his shirt collar.

The plainclothes cop stood by, a sour expression on his face. "Come on in," he said dryly, lifting up the yellow tape, indicating that JR should duck under it.

After disengaging Carmen's arms from around his neck, he went under the tape. Then he took her hand as the cop led the two of them over to the side, behind a clothes rack and away from the prying eyes of onlookers. JR wanted to know what was up. Was Carmen a suspect? Was he needed here as her long-time friend or as a lawyer?

As soon as they stopped moving, Carmen released his hand and threw her arms around him again, resuming the position of head buried in neck. The policeman stood by, obviously not pleased but trying for patience. "Um, miss…I need to talk to you some more."

JR stroked her hair, murmuring, "Baby. It's okay."

"Now," the cop insisted.

"Carmen. Come on. You need to help the police."

With a loud sniffle, she pulled away from his embrace, nodding. "Okay. Sure."

JR produced one of his snowy-white handkerchiefs and offered it to her. She took it with a grateful smile. Even with mascara-smeared cheeks, her small, elegant nose red from crying, her lids puffy and her streaky blond hair in need of a comb, she was still the most beautiful woman he had ever known.

And, as it had for years when he gazed at her, his heart turned over in his chest with an all-too-familiar, painful thud. Unrequited love was the pits.

He turned his attention to the cop. "Officer, what is it exactly you need from Ms. Coyle?"

"That's Detective," the cop said in a deep, rich voice that made JR wonder if he was a singer in his spare time. "Detective Marshall." He fished around in an inner suit pocket and came up with a business card, which he handed to JR.

"Macklin Thurgood Marshall, Jr.," JR read aloud. He raised an eyebrow. "I'm impressed."

"And you are…?"

"Stanton Fitzgerald Ewing, JR to pretty much everybody," he told the older man, withdrawing his silver card case and handing one of his law firm's business cards to Marshall.

As the older man glanced at his card, JR could tell the moment he noticed the *Esq.* after his name, because an expression of displeasure crossed his coffee-colored features. JR had seen it before—yet one more protector of the people's safety who was not thrilled with yet one more protector of the people's rights. Marshall slipped his card into one of his pants pockets, then, having decided to deal with him instead of a teary woman, said, "Look, Counselor, I have Ms. Coyle's preliminary statement, but we need to talk to her some more."

"Is she a suspect? Does she need a lawyer? Because I was on the phone with her when the shots occurred and I can vouch for—"

Marshall interrupted him with an impatient wave of his hand. "No, she told us all about that, and she's been cleared. We just need her statement to be as complete as possible, and she's obviously in no shape to cooperate with us now. Tomorrow morning will be fine."

All right, then, JR thought with a mental sigh of relief. Carmen wasn't in trouble. This time, anyway. He put a finger under her chin and lifted it, so he could look into her eyes. "Okay with you?"

She nodded, then sniffled.

"Come home with me now?" he added.

She nodded again, grateful tears brimming above her lower lashes, then leaned against him. JR turned his attention back to the detective, his arm firmly around Carmen's shoulders. "We'll be there in the morning. How's nine?"

"Fine."

Marshall ushered them down the escalator and out the employee entrance so they could avoid the crowds. JR kept his arm around Carmen the whole time, escorting her to his car. As he did, he used his free hand to call his secretary on his cell, instructing her to put off the last two appointments of the day and the first one in the morning. He was a patent and intellectual property rights lawyer who worked in a large firm; none of the appointments were emergencies or he'd have had one of his associates take care of them.

He opened the passenger door for Carmen and watched her get in and buckle her seat belt. "Where'd you park your car?"

She shook her head. "I sold it. I took the bus here."

"You sold your car?"

"Yes." She leaned back against the headrest and closed her eyes. The skin around her mouth and eyes was white. She'd really been through it, he thought, hurting for her as though it had happened to him.

But...she'd sold her car? he thought, walking around to the driver's side. He frowned but knew now wasn't the time to question her further. What would she do for transportation? he wondered. Los Angeles and the surrounding environs were not friendly to carless citizens.

In silence, they headed away from the Westside mall and made their way toward his condo in Santa Monica. Carmen opened her eyes when they pulled into the underground parking lot, took JR's arm as they rode the elevator up to the seventh floor, and the moment he opened the door, hurried right over to the large picture window that faced the ocean. Hugging herself, she stood there, staring out at the cloudless blue sky of early autumn, at the late afternoon surf, the tall palm trees, the joggers, dog-walkers, tourists moving along the palisades that overlooked the beaches below.

She loved this view, had often teased him about how their friendship was contingent upon his continuing to live in this Ocean Boulevard condo, so she could look out his window. There was something, she would say, about the pristine, picture-postcard prettiness of his view that made her feel clean and calm in a way that nothing else did.

"Do you want a shot of something?" he asked her. "Brandy?"

She turned around, her expression wistful. "Hot tea?"

"I think I can rustle some up."

By the time he got back with her cup of hot tea and

a plateful of her favorite cookies—which he kept in the house for when she visited—Carmen was curled up in her usual place at one corner of his large couch. Her feet were bare; her rubber thongs were on the floor being sniffed at by Owl, his aging tomcat. The Nordstrom shopping bag rested against the sofa.

Noting that Carmen was trembling, JR pulled the afghan off the back of the couch and covered her up to her chin, tucking it behind her shoulders and over her bare feet. As he did, she offered a sad, tired smile. "You're the best."

"Drink some tea," he said.

She reached an arm out from under the afghan and took a sip.

He lowered himself onto the adjacent armchair and leaned over, with his elbows on his knees and his hands clasped between his legs to keep himself from sitting next to her and pulling her into his arms again. She aroused all kinds of protective feelings in him, but if he gave in to them whenever he experienced them, how would he ever get on with his life? "Better?"

She took another sip of the hot liquid and nodded. "At least I don't have to pay for the suit."

It was one of Carmen's classic non sequiturs, but he was used to the way she leaped from subject to subject, often without verbal signals to let the listener in on the fact that she was doing so. "Suit?"

"Remember I was trying on a business suit when we were talking? I used the jacket to try to stop the bleeding." At the last word, she began to tremble again and had to put the cup down. "Oh, God, the blood, JR. I was covered with it. They let me wash up and put on my own clothes before they interviewed me. I'm not used to seeing real, live blood. I mean, you know, outside of a movie or TV show."

"Yeah, that must have been rough."

She rubbed her hands together, blew on them, then picked up the cup again. "The poor woman. They wouldn't tell me her name."

"They'll release that information after they've notified her relatives. What happened? Do you want to talk about it? I mean, can you talk about it?"

She took another sip then set the cup down and pulled the blanket more tightly around her slim body. "No. It's okay. I think he used a silencer."

"Did you see him? The shooter?"

"Only a glimpse from the back." Her brow furrowed. "Actually I don't know if it was a he." He watched her face, usually so lively—not now, of course—and always so expressive that you never had to guess at what Carmen was feeling. "It could have been one of those really athletic women. Nowadays, it's kind of hard to tell, you know?"

He waited as her brow furrowed some more in thought. "The sound," she went on after a while, "the silencer. It wasn't like a gunshot, but kind of a popping noise. And then there was this smell."

"Graphite."

"Yeah, that's what Mac said."

"Mac would be Macklin Thurgood Marshall, Jr., I take it."

"Some name, huh?" Her smile was a ghost of its usual open and joyous self, but it was, at least, a smile. "Like the Supreme Court justice."

"Thurgood Marshall," JR said. "The first African American to sit on the court. He was a pretty great man."

She nodded. "I remember. Anyhow, Mac said that, about the graphite." Out of nowhere, her eyes filled again. "Oh, JR. I felt so…helpless." The tears brimmed over and slid down her cheeks.

Again, he ordered himself to stay right where he was. Which did him no good whatsoever because years of conditioning, years of taking care of and comforting Carmen, were just too ingrained. He moved onto the couch and gathered her up in his arms, even pulled her onto his lap. As usual, she buried her face in his neck and he smelled her hair, always clean and with a subtle lime scent from the herbal shampoo she used. Her body was long and lean, but there were soft places, lots of them, and he exerted all the discipline he'd honed over the years to keep his own body's reactions to a minimum.

"It was so awful," she whispered.

"I know, baby."

He wanted to hear the entire story, from beginning to end, but that could wait for later. He held her some more, let her cry, almost felt like crying himself. When Carmen hurt, so did he.

After a while, she lifted her head and gazed at him. "I'm sorry."

"For what?"

"Falling apart on you." She moved off his lap and curled up into the corner of the couch again.

He stared at her in disbelief. "You just tried to save the life of a murdered woman. If anyone has the right to fall apart, I'd say it's you."

"No, I need to be stronger. You told me I needed to be stronger and you were right."

For a moment, he blanked. "When did I say that?"

"The other night, remember? When I was whining about Tio and how I had no idea he'd been dealing? And how it just about broke my heart when my landlady came to the door asking for the back rent? Remember? And you told me that I sucked when it came to choosing men, and that I needed to grow up and start to take responsibility for myself, and needed to get a real job, and that I was on the verge of being pathetic?"

He groaned. "Did I really say all that? That you were pathetic?"

"On the verge, you said. And yes, that was the very word. Pathetic." The look on her tear-streaked face now was earnest and not at all accusatory. "You said that what had been sort of cute when I was younger wasn't cute anymore. Remember?"

He winced. "Ouch."

Oh, yes, JR remembered, and he felt like a bastard. Damn. Had he really been so harsh with her? But he knew the answer. He had. He'd already made up his mind that he had to end their connection before he lost whatever chance he had at happiness, so he'd decided to let her have it with both barrels. He'd given Carmen—whom he'd known, it felt like all his life—a no-holds-barred talking-to. He'd listed her crimes: always arriving late for appointments, forgetting to return library books, letting her cell phone messages pile up so no one could get through, borrowing money and taking forever to pay it back, running out of gas because the gauge was broken and she'd forget to have it fixed.

He'd spared her nothing. He'd told her that all of that behavior was getting old and that she'd only gotten away with this stuff because of her sweet personality and the fact that she never capitalized on her beauty.

That last part, the reference to her beauty, she'd protested heartily because she was honestly unaware of just how attractive she was. Which amazed him; hell, all she needed to do was look in the mirror and there it was. But still. She was that rarity. A naturally lovely woman without vanity or self-absorption or a sense of entitlement. Also without much self-worth. But one with a kind heart.

Also, he was discovering, a stout one.

In short, the one woman in the world for him.

But his feelings for her weren't returned. He'd approached it, kiddingly, over the years. "Hey, Carm, what's your view on best friends falling in love?" "Hey, Carm, ever thought about the two of us? You know, later on down the line when we've had our flings with people we'll never marry and are ready to settle down?"

And she'd laughed and told him to stop kidding with her; or told him she wasn't in his league and he could do a lot better; or told him that boyfriends were easy to find, a good friend much rarer. All those little sayings women came up with when they just weren't into a guy.

She liked bad boys, destructive creeps who reeked of mindless testosterone and who were good for the short run only. Maybe it had to do with that low self-esteem and her image of herself as being not quite good enough to fit into her brainy, high-achieving family, but really, who cared why?

Facts were facts. It wasn't going to happen between the two of them.

JR knew his looks were okay, his testosterone level healthy, that he'd attracted his fair share of interesting, interested women over the years. But, basically, he was just too straight-arrow for Carmen. He wasn't given to sneering or dressing all in black or letting his beard grow just enough to look as though he need a shave but didn't care. She was plainly and simply not into him, on a man-woman level, at least. Oh, she loved him, would give her life for him. As a friend.

And the other night, when he'd finally decided to break her hold on him, he'd let it rip. He'd been paternal and judgmental and, yeah, unkind. Maybe he'd wanted to drive her away. Whatever his motives, she'd heard him, taken it in, had not been in the least offended. She'd actually thanked him.

"Carm," he told her now, "you can grow up tomorrow. You saw a woman die today and it's okay to need comfort for that."

"You sure?" Huge brown eyes, sad eyes, unsure-of-herself eyes, gazed at him, asking for permission.

"I'm sure."

"Okay, then." She offered up a weak smile. "Just for today, I'll let you pamper me. I still have to get a job. But I'll do a Scarlett O'Hara and deal with it tomorrow." She yawned and then stretched. "Right now, I think I have to take a nap."

He got up from the couch and watched as she stretched out and pulled the afghan up over herself. "Will you call Shannon?" she asked with another yawn. "Tell my sister what happened and not to worry and that I'm okay?"

"Sure."

In a matter of seconds, she was fast asleep.

He stood over her a while longer and watched her, watched as the late afternoon shadows crossed her lovely face and made the pale blond streaks in her hair—all natural—glisten white. Watched her tremble occasionally, as though dreaming of something fearful.

And as he gazed at her, he felt that strong, soul-deep ache that he associated with Carmen only, felt the yearning to make love to her, to take her pain from her and let it be his. It was a yearning so deep it was as if a chunk of him didn't belong to himself, but only to her, to this woman who called him friend.

Chapter 2

As they sat side by side on a bench at the West L.A. police station, Carmen took a sip of awful coffee and glanced over at JR's profile. He had such a nice face. More than nice, actually. As he'd aged, he'd grown quite handsome. His hair was thick and light brown, worn short. His eyes were the nicest pale blue. His English ancestry—family lore had it that he was descended from royalty—was evident in the high-bridged, finely chiseled nose, the firm jawline and thin mouth. As she took in the expensive, gold-rimmed eyeglasses he wore, suddenly she remembered another pair of glasses—bottle-thick with black frames and truly ugly.

He'd been wearing them the day she'd met him, twenty-two years ago. She was seven and he was eight, a friend of her older sister's. Shannon, who was always adopting misfits, had dragged him home with her from their school for brainy kids. He'd sure been one of those—dorky, nerdy, skinny and just loaded with brains.

He still had the brains, of course, but the other adjectives no longer applied. Today, he was wearing one of his beautifully cut suits, this one charcoal-gray with a pale gray shirt and matching tie. She'd never been a woman who liked men in suits, but with JR she made an exception.

She noticed a tiny nick on his chin where he must have cut himself shaving. She licked a finger and rubbed the redness away.

"What are you doing?" he asked, startled.

"Cleaning you up, so nothing can take away from your gorgeousness."

"Cut it out," he said good-naturedly.

Smiling to herself, grateful she'd been able to get her mind off yesterday's tragedy, even for a moment, Carmen took another sip of the disgusting police coffee. She was not a morning person and would take all the help she could get in waking up.

Detective Marshall appeared from behind the reception desk and motioned Carmen and JR to come with him. He looked even more tired today, she thought, noting the deep lines around his mouth and the way his shoulders slumped in his well-worn suit jacket, this one a dark plaid. He led the way down a hallway and into a large room filled with desks set at odd angles.

His was piled with folders and paperwork and a few family pictures in frames, which she didn't get a chance to examine before he indicated she should sit in the visitor chair adjacent to his desk. Then he went to another work station and brought over a chair for JR.

As he did, he said, in that really cool, deep voice of his, "Counselor, I have some regards for you."

JR noticed a subtle lessening of yesterday's thinly veiled hostile attitude on the part of the detective and wondered what had caused it. "Really?"

"Yeah. A buddy of mine, Jacob Johnson, knows you. Said you used to be a deputy D.A. before you took on your present job. He also says you were really helpful with his dad. George Frederick Johnson? You helped get him into the VA."

"Of course. George. How is he doing?"

"Better. They got him on meds now, so he's not violent anymore." He turned to Carmen. "Your boyfriend here, he kept my friend's dad out of jail, wouldn't take any payment."

"Hey," JR said with an embarrassed shrug. "The man served his country."

He was about to go on to correct the impression that he was Carmen's boyfriend, when she popped in instead with, "Isn't JR the very best? I mean, how many lawyers do you know who donate their time like he does?"

"Not too many," Mac concurred. "But there are some. Which is why I'm not one hundred percent prejudiced against the breed."

"Just ninety-eight percent," JR countered wryly.

"Something like that." Mac favored them with a small, cynical cop smile, then went on. "Okay, now, let's get down to business." He took a document from a wire basket and handed it to Carmen. "We have witness statements but, frankly, they don't add up to much. You were the closest to the actual murder. This is the statement you gave us yesterday. Would you mind looking it over, seeing if there's anything you want to add?"

As Carmen was perusing the statement, JR asked Mac, "Have you made any progress?"

He paused before saying, "I don't generally talk about open cases to civilians." After another moment's hesitation, he went on. "But in your case, I'll make an exception." He shrugged. "Which doesn't amount to much because we've got nothing. We've got eyewitnesses, all with a slightly different version of what Ms. Coyle, here, says. A body rushing by, all in black, bill pulled down over face, dark hair, maybe, or no hair."

He shrugged again. "After that, we've got one sure it was a woman, two positive it was a man, one saying it was a young man—late teens—another sure it was an older guy. Height anywhere from five-six to six feet. One thought there was a letter on the cap, but couldn't remember the letter—another sure there wasn't. Even if we could bring in a suspect or two, we won't be able to put together a lineup." He rubbed his tired eyes. "The gun, a twenty-two caliber, and the silencer were found in a garbage bin a block from the mall, no fingerprints."

Carmen glanced up from her reading. "What was her name? The woman who died?"

"Can't let that out yet. Her husband is in the Marines, serving in Iraq, and we haven't been able to reach him."

"So, she was married," she said sadly. "Her poor husband. Did she have kids?"

"No."

"Well, at least…"

Instead of finishing her sentence, she went back to studying the report while the two men watched her.

After a moment or two she raised her head again. "I'd say the running figure was shorter rather than taller, but apart from that..." She raised then lowered a shoulder. "It all happened so fast."

"How short?" Mac asked.

"Closer to my height—five-seven or -eight."

He made a note. "Well, that's something, anyway. Did you notice the victim earlier? I mean, did you see her while you were shopping, you know, looking through the racks?"

"No."

"So you wouldn't have noticed if she seemed nervous, like someone was following her, anything like that?"

"No, again. Sorry."

"How long had you been in the dressing room?"

"I guess five minutes or so. I had tried on one suit and I hated it, and tried on another and then I called JR and complained." She looked over at him with a quick smile of apology, then told Mac, "Five to seven minutes."

He nodded. "The victim must have been there about the same amount of time. She'd tried on two items. Did you hear her go into the dressing room?"

"No. I didn't even know anyone was next door until I heard the sound. The gunshot. Well, more of a gun pop."

JR had a question of his own he wanted to ask. "Do you think it was done by a professional?"

"Most likely," Mac answered. "But we have no idea why. The vic, well, we've talked to her sister and there is no reason anyone can think of for the attack on her. Married a year. Quiet. Didn't screw around. Churchgoing. Worked for the county. Nothing controversial.

We're digging some more—maybe the husband'll know something. There has to be a reason for a hit."

"A hit?" Carmen asked. "You mean like murder for hire?"

"It was done by a pro, I'm pretty sure. Nothing spur of the moment. Carefully planned. Must have followed her into the store, didn't want to take a chance in the crowd, waited 'til she was in the dressing room, followed her, got her there. And after that, from what we can tell, the shooter walked quickly through the store, down the escalator, and was gone, all before we were even called in." He frowned and blew out an impatient breath. "Can you think of anything else, anything at all?"

All of this talk about the woman's murder was making Carmen feel kind of sad and fragile again, but she wanted to help as much as she could, so she closed her eyes and tried to concentrate. Something had occurred to her yesterday while she sat on the floor outside the dressing room. What was it? She tried and tried, but it wouldn't come up. Maybe if she didn't think about it, it would surface.

She opened her eyes and shook her head apologetically. "Sorry."

Mac stood, indicating the interview was over. "Well, thanks for your help," he said, shaking first her hand, then JR's. "If you think of anything else, you know where to reach me."

Outside in the autumn sunshine, as cars whizzed by on Santa Monica Boulevard, Carmen drew in a large breath and let it out, wishing she could shake the sad feeling. "Oh, JR," she said.

"What?"

"It's awful the way one little thing can alter everything else. You know?" She gazed up at her friend, feeling quite emotional as she tried to explain. "You're walking along the street and minding your own business and all of a sudden you decide to turn a corner and everything's different then. Your whole life is different. I mean, I hate that I chose that dressing room, that I was next door to that poor woman. I hate that the poor woman died. I hate that I couldn't save her. I hate that it happened at all," she finished sadly, "and that's the truth."

"Yeah." JR's blue-eyed gaze behind gold rims was sympathetic. "And I hate that I can't fix it for you."

"You can't." She poked her index finger into his chest. "And you shouldn't, anyway," she said, trying to lighten up. "I have to fix myself, remember? Before I become 'pathetic'?"

He raised his gaze to the heavens. "Are you ever going to let me forget what I said?"

"Nope," she replied. "It was a life-altering moment and needs to be commemorated. So, can I buy you breakfast?"

He glanced at his watch. "I have to be in court in half an hour."

"Oh. Darn. I wanted to take you out. To thank you."

"I ate early, while you were sleeping. And with what money?"

"I have money," she said, suddenly feeling a little defensive. "Well, some. That's why I sold my car. I had to have something to live on until I get work and can pay Mom and Shannon back."

"What if you need your car to get to work?"

"There's such a thing as taking the bus." She smiled. "We common folk do it all the time, you know."

He didn't want to play. "I do know that. I also know L.A. is not known for her superior mass transit system. What if you have to spend hours waiting for a connection? What if you have to come home late at night?" He shook his head, obviously disapproving of yet one more of Carmen's decisions, one more time thinking her a fool.

She felt herself bristling. Okay, maybe she shouldn't have sold her car before thinking through her options, but she didn't really want to hear a lecture at the moment, especially not from JR. Not today.

In fact, she was getting a little tired of being lectured.

"Look," she said, still defensive and now irritated also, "go on to court, okay? Thanks for being with me this morning," she added, then walked off.

He caught up to her. "Where are you headed? I can drop you off."

"I'm going to the storefront, then home. Shannon insists on seeing me, to make sure I'm okay. It's out of your way."

"It's not out of my way. The courthouse is right near there." He took her elbow. "Come on."

Like JR, Shannon Coyle was a successful lawyer employed by a large, prestigious L.A. firm. But the Coyle children had been raised with an awareness of the haves and the have-nots. They'd been taught to give back to the community, and to always look out for those less fortunate. So a few months ago, after she'd received her share of a huge multimillion-dollar settlement against a chemical firm that had been dumping toxins into the Pacific Ocean, Shannon had decided to honor the lesson of their childhood. She'd pleaded with, bullied and coerced a couple of other lawyer friends—JR being one—to donate a few hours a week each, and had set up shop in a small, shabby storefront on Pacific Avenue in Venice, open mornings only for now. Here, the homeless, the disenfranchised, those unable to work the legal system to right injustice, were welcomed and counseled and sometimes even helped.

It was here, at the storefront, that Carmen had been ordered by her older sister to show up. The minute JR ushered Carmen through the door, Shannon came barreling out of the single rear office, arms thrown wide. Even though she was shorter than Carmen by at least seven inches, she hugged her younger sister with enough intensity to more than make up for her lack of height. JR watched as Carmen closed her eyes and let Shannon embrace her with all the ferocity of a mamma bear.

They had little in common physically. Shannon was not only short, she was also just a bit plump, with dark brown hair. Carmen was tall and lean and blond. They had the same eyes, though, the Coyle eyes. A warm, rich brown, with a fringe of long lashes and perfectly arched eyebrows. And they'd always been as close as two sisters could be. Over the years, JR had marveled at their bond. He'd been an only child. A lonely child.

Shannon pulled away and studied Carmen's face. "Sweetie, are you okay?"

"I'm fine, Shan."

"You sure?"

"Sure."

The receptionist, a round, middle-aged Latina named Guadalupe Delgado—Lupe—who ran the place with a gentle but iron fist, stood in front of her desk now, waiting for Shannon to release her sister, so she, too, could draw Carmen into a warm, loving hug.

JR was always amazed at how much *touching* the Coyles and their friends engaged in. His own home had been more formal. Touching was brief, and for special times only. Meeting the Coyle sisters all those years ago, had opened up all kinds of new worlds to him.

Lupe smelled like warm cinnamon, Carmen thought, reveling in her embrace. And walnuts. She must have been baking this morning.

She loved Lupe like an aunt, but just last week, she'd been too embarrassed to face her. Lupe was her landlady, and it had been the older woman's visit, informing Carmen that the rent was three months overdue, that had begun the whole nightmare of cleaning up after Tio. But the rent was paid now, Lupe had told her not to worry anymore, and they were back to being close friends, thank heaven.

"Excuse me, ladies," she heard JR say. "I don't mean to interrupt the lovefest, but I'm off."

Carmen withdrew from Lupe's warm hug, but avoided looking at him as she mumbled, "Thanks again for everything."

"When will we see you again, JR?" Lupe asked, then walked over to her desk and peered at the appointment book lying open on it. "You're on Wednesday mornings, right? So we'll see you tomorrow."

"Correct. Hey, Carm, take care of yourself, okay?"

She knew he was looking right at her, but she still felt kind of, well, unsettled after their brief flare-up outside the West L.A. police headquarters. "I'll do my best," she said, still not meeting his gaze.

He waited a moment more—probably for her to turn around, to tell him everything between them was okay, which she pointedly did not do because she had no idea how things were between them—before walking out the door.

After he did, she turned to watch him go.

His suit really did fit him well, Carmen couldn't help observing. Even though he was over six feet, you couldn't call JR a *big* man; he'd been a skinny kid and was still kind of lean. But she'd seen him in workout clothing and bathing trunks, and he had a nicely muscled body, with long runner's legs. Of course, you couldn't really see the body in the suit today; what you saw was his elegance, that born-to-a-life-of-privilege ease of movement that came so naturally to him.

And why, she wondered, was she, out of nowhere, thinking about JR's body? Hadn't she, just seconds ago, been kind of pissed off at him?

"He's one of the good guys, isn't he?" Shannon remarked.

Startled out of her reverie, Carmen looked to her left. Her sister was standing there, arms crossed, also checking out JR. "Sure is," she had to agree. "He's about the best friend a girl could have."

"That he is."

"And he's always been there for me. I'm going to make it up to him—all the years of him taking care of me. I'm going to change all that."

Shannon turned and gazed up at her, head cocked to one side, reminding Carmen, as she always had, of a busy, intelligent bird. "And how do you plan to do that?"

"By—" she shrugged "—you know, not needing him so much. By acting like a grown-up."

Shannon raised an eyebrow. "A grown-up? My, my." She returned her gaze to JR, just as he was getting into his Lexus. "I wonder how he'll take that?"

"He'll be relieved, of course."

"Really?"

"Why wouldn't he be?"

"It's a two-way street, you know, this caretaker business. There's the caretaker and the one being taken care of. Both get something out of it. If you decide to change the rules, I wonder how JR will react?"

"He'll love it, trust me," Carmen said earnestly. "It's time, Shannon. He told me so himself. It's obvious he considers me nothing but a pain in the butt."

Frowning, Shannon studied her sister for a couple of silent moments before saying skeptically, "Are you serious?"

"Yes."

"You think, you truly think, that JR, our JR, considers you nothing but a pain in the butt? Do you honestly not know?"

"Not know what?" Again, her lots-smaller-but-two-years-older sister stared at her, head cocked to the other side now. "Not know what?" Carmen repeated.

Shaking her head, Shannon walked back toward her office, muttering, "Never mind."

Carmen followed her. "What?"

"Hey, if you don't know, it's not up to me to tell you."

"Shan, I think I may have to strangle you. Now tell me. What are you talking about? What don't I know?"

Shannon stopped inside her office, motioned Carmen in, then closed the door behind them. She stared at her and seemed to be considering something for a moment or two before finally throwing up her hands. "For God's sake, the man's in love with you."

Her sister's shocking statement made Carmen's mouth drop open. Now it was her turn to stare, which she did for several speechless moments before shaking her head, first slowly, then more rapidly. "No, he's not."

"Yes, he is. Has been for years."

"No, no." Carmen couldn't seem to stop shaking her head. She needed to push away the entire concept, push it far, far away…even as a tiny voice in the back of her mind was whispering that this wasn't really news, was it?

She ordered the voice to shut up. "Not possible."

"Why?" Shannon stood, hands on hips, one knowing eyebrow arched.

Mind reeling, Carmen walked over to the small window that faced the street and peered out. JR was just driving away. "Well, because he's never said anything."

She whirled around and faced her sister. "And, I mean, why would he be in love with me? The idea is absolutely—" she fought to find the right word "—ludicrous! He can have *anyone,* college graduates, sophisticated Ph.D.s with two-hundred-dollar haircuts. Remember Sarah? And that…what was her name? Eloise? He could have them, women like them. *Has* had them. What in the world would he want with me?"

Shannon's expression as she listened to Carmen's sputtered protests was an all-too-familiar combination of impatience and compassion. Each of her family members had looked at her in the same way over the years. "Stop it, Carmen. Don't do that to yourself," she said firmly. "Don't put yourself down. When are you going to get that you are every bit as valuable as ten Sarahs and fifteen Eloises?"

She jutted her chin out. "I'm not putting myself down, I'm just stating the truth. JR and I are way too different for him to feel that way about me. And for me to feel that way about him. End of discussion."

Feeling defensive, not for the first time this morning, and deeply uncomfortable with this entire discussion, she stalked over to the small table that stood against the far wall, studied the African violet she'd given Shannon as an office-warming gift, then picked off some of the brown leaves.

She stuck her finger in the soil. "This needs water," she snapped, perhaps a bit more harshly than the situation warranted. "And better light."

She hurried over to the bottled-water stand, filled a paper cup, walked back to the plant, sprinkled a few drops on the leaves and poured the rest of the liquid on the soil.

This had been another of her jobs—tending plants at a huge local nursery, a job she'd really liked but had to quit because the manager kept rubbing himself up against her and wouldn't stop, even when she told him to. And, yeah, she should have filed some kind of harassment complaint, but, hey, it was too much trouble. Carmen hated trouble.

"You should get some more plants in here," she told Shannon. "The place needs cheering up."

"Fine. Tell Lupe what kind we should get."

"I'll do it for you."

"Even better. You go get some plants for us and I'll reimburse you."

"No, you won't," Carmen said firmly. "I owe you money."

"And I told you you don't have to pay me back."

"And I told you I do."

This was not the first time they'd had this particular exchange and probably wouldn't be the last. Carmen folded her arms across her chest and stood her ground.

Narrowing her gaze, Shannon seemed to study her sister before shrugging, as though giving up on a hopeless cause. "Fine. Whatever."

Carmen didn't like being dismissed so cavalierly and was about to say so when the sound of the outside door jingling announced that they had a visitor. Shannon walked briskly out of her office; Carmen followed.

A young woman who couldn't have been more than twenty-two or -three stood in the reception area with two nursery-school-aged children. Her face was badly bruised; one eye was swollen shut and her upper lip was red and puffy.

Lupe smiled at her. "May I help you?"

The woman seemed both shy and scared. "I was told that, um, I mean, my friend said…"

Shannon walked over to her and held out her hand. "Shannon Coyle," she said with a welcoming smile, shaking the young woman's hand. "I'm a lawyer and your friend was right. What can we do for you?"

Lupe piped up. "Shannon, we need paperwork filled out first."

Shannon waved her away. "We'll do all that later.

Why don't you and your kids come into my office," she said to the woman, "and tell me all about it."

Lupe opened her desk drawer and took out a tin, then followed them into the office. "How would you children like some freshly baked cookies?"

After the door closed behind them, Carmen stood there staring at it, feeling abandoned, for some stupid reason. All kinds of thoughts and emotions roiled around inside her. Anger at whomever had beaten up the poor young mother. Admiration for Shannon…and just a tinge of envy, which she'd had all her life, it seemed. Naturally warm and smart as could be, with all that legal education, her sister had always been at the top of her class.

Carmen admired Lupe, too—she was hardworking and determined. The daughter of immigrants, she'd saved her money and owned real estate. She gave her time to help others, always had cookies for the kids and was good with paperwork.

Who was Carmen? And what did she have to recommend her? A high school education, never even near the top of her class. No real purpose in life, no goals to work toward. She was impulsive, had always had trouble staying with anything for long, had a terrible history with men, was too trusting, was always needing to be bailed out of stupid situations she'd gotten herself into. She had no savings, not even a car.

Granted, the list was one-sided. She did have *some* positive qualities, a talent or two. But they were minor. The fact was her life so far had not exactly been admirable. This was not a pretty picture, and it was rare that she forced herself to look at it. JR's lecture had been the catalyst.

Speaking of JR...

When Carmen thought of Shannon's declaration, she actually laughed. JR in love with her? Nonsense. She'd never heard a more absurd statement in her life.

She was sitting in the bleachers watching JR train for a marathon race by doing laps. It was a beautiful, warm day, with lots of overhead sunshine and not a cloud in sight. JR was dressed in running shorts and a sleeveless T-shirt; his long, tan, muscled legs and arms were all shiny with perspiration, and as he passed her, he glanced over at her with a grin.

Then, as though suddenly remembering something, he stopped running and turned to face her. Hands on hips, his posture all male confidence and pride, he gazed at her, his expression serious now...and really hot. *Look at me,* it said. *Look at what you could have.* And she found her gaze wandering from the top of his hair, all mussed and sexy from his workout, over the chiseled bones of his face, glowing and slick with sweat, down past his neck and his soaked T-shirt to the area just below the waistband of his shorts.

As her gaze came to rest there, on the nicely rounded bulge between his legs, he grinned again, a sly, knowing grin. Check it out, babe, he said. It's yours if you want it.

Only now he wasn't JR. He was Tio.

And the look on his face wasn't sly or sexy, it was crude and arrogant.

The sun disappeared behind a huge, gray cloud, and all the joy went out of the day. Tio left the track, coming toward her, kicking over some sports equipment as he did, making way too much noise. Everyone in the stands was looking at her and she hated it. Tio kept coming, kept kicking all kinds of things as he did—saw horses and punching bags and huge, metal storage bins. A dog growled, then began to bark, a high-pitched, truly annoying and truly terrifying bark. And over that was another sound. Someone knocking. Knocking. Knocking…

Carmen sat up in bed, her heart racing. What? Where was she?

"Carmen!" The voice came from outside her front door. It was a woman's voice, and the dog kept barking. Bonzo was the dog's name and it was Gidget who was calling her.

Scrambling out of bed, Carmen checked to make sure she was wearing something, which she was. Most nights she slept nude, but tonight she had on an old pair of pajamas because the weather had turned cold. She ran across the floor to the front door, calling out, "Gidget? Is that you?"

"Yes. Are you okay?"

Flicking the switch for the outdoor porch light, Carmen opened the door to see the tiny, wrinkled, white-haired, homeless woman whom she considered her friend looking at her with grave concern. A shaggy brown mutt stood by her side, his tongue lolling out of the side of his mouth.

"I'm fine," Carmen said. "Hey, Bonzo. Come on in, both of you."

Always, Carmen asked, but always, Gidget refused; she was one of those people who couldn't tolerate being inside four walls. Her shopping cart and the oversize cardboard box she called home were situated in the narrow alleyway that ran from the front door of Carmen's one-room cottage to the street.

"Nah," Gidget said, pulling the thick Native American blanket she usually wore tightly around her shoulders. "I just wanted to make sure you were okay."

Hugging herself against the chill, Carmen looked down the alleyway, dimly lit by the yellow porch light. "What was all that noise?"

"Someone was tryin' to break in to your place. Didn't you hear 'em?"

For the first time since opening her eyes, Carmen came fully awake. "What are you talking about?"

"Someone, a stranger, couldn't see the face, was at your door, sniffin' around your windows. Good thing Bonzo woke up, scared him off." The elderly woman chuckled. "'Bout killed himself trippin' over the garbage cans."

The shiver that went all through her had nothing to do with the cold. "Did you see who it was? Are you sure it was a man?"

Gidget shrugged. "Couldn't tell. They wore black, had a baseball cap on, is all. Bonzo saw 'em, but dogs can't talk, now can they?"

Black. Baseball cap. No. She really didn't want to hear that.

Carmen bent over and stroked the dog's soft head. "Thanks, Bonzo. I really appreciate it."

The shaggy brown mutt gave her a doggy grin.

Gidget backed off the porch. "You go back to bed now," she said.

"Can I get you a glass of water? Some crackers?"

"We're fine," the woman said, turning around and walking away, the dog following right behind.

"Thanks again, Gidget," Carmen called after her

before closing the door and double-locking it. Then she ran around the room, turning on every light in the place before heading into the small kitchen to make herself a cup of tea.

The dream came back to her. It had been about JR, of all people. Because Shannon had put a ridiculous idea into her head. And then JR had turned into Tio.

And a black-clad figure wearing a baseball cap had tried to break in.

All of which didn't have to mean a thing, she told herself. And she needed to stop shaking. Tea. The reason she was standing in the kitchen. Hot tea would help. She filled the kettle, put it on the stove.

Hugging herself, she wandered out of the kitchen and gazed around the room, taking in the mixture of family hand-me-downs and thrift-store rescues, throw rugs, pillows of varying fabrics and colors, many of which she'd made or embroidered herself, piles of CDs on the floor, some artwork by friends on the walls. Her little nest, her own little tiny, ramshackle house with its postage-stamp-size rear garden in the not-so-nice part of Venice, fifteen blocks from the ocean. She loved it here.

And someone had tried to invade it. Someone dressed in black.

Another involuntary shiver took hold of her body.

Carmen had always felt safe here. No more—that feeling was gone. Without thinking, she tore off her pajamas and put on a pair of sweats and old tennies, hunted down her purse and felt around in her purse for her car keys. She needed to get out of here, take a drive, go somewhere other than here, where she didn't feel safe.

And then she remembered. She had no car.

The sound of the whistling teakettle made her jump.

Her heart was beating way too quickly. She was terrified. Scared to death.

And she had no idea what to do about it.

Chapter 3

JR glanced at his watch. Nine-fifteen in the morning. He'd been at work since seven, catching up, and would have to leave for the Venice storefront in a few minutes. But before he did, he wanted to check in on Carmen, see how she was doing. After he punched in her home number, he let it ring several times, but when the answering machine switched on, he didn't leave word. Instead, he called her cell phone.

She answered right away. "Hi, JR."

"How are you doing, Carm?"

"I'm okay."

"Just okay?"

"You know…"

She was not okay, he could hear it in her voice, in her lack of energy. Carmen was, by nature, pretty upbeat. Even if things weren't going well, she usually tried to act as if everything was just fine. That she wasn't even making an effort today meant it was bad.

It was going to take her a while to get over witnessing a murder.

"Hey, Carm," he said, more quietly now, "Monday was a rough day. I'm here if you need me."

"Thanks."

He waited for more than "thanks." But there was nothing. No "Oh, JR. I'm so sad and I need a friend." No suggestion he come over tonight for pasta, or that they take a stroll together on the Venice boardwalk so she could shake the blues, or head down to Hermosa Beach to catch some jazz or any of the myriad ways they'd socialized over the years, cheering each other up in down times, celebrating in up times.

Not today. Just…nothing.

He kept his tone casual as he said, "So, what's on the agenda?"

"I'm about to get on a bus."

He could practically see her shrugging listlessly. Again, he waited for an explanation, but she remained silent. This was troubling; there was never silence between them, never. Sure, Carmen usually did most of the talking and he the listening, but it worked well for them that way. Not now. Was she mad at him? Was it because he'd given her grief about selling her car? Yes, he knew it was her business how she got around town and not his. Although, he also knew he was right—she'd just made getting a job, navigating the sprawl that was Los Angeles and its environs, much, much harder.

Dial it back, he told himself. He was doing it again, thinking of Carmen in a protective way. Paternal, even.

Filled with advice. She wasn't his child, his job or his responsibility.

He glanced out the window of his office. He wasn't senior enough to have a corner with an ocean view, but at least there were mountains to gaze at, the ones beyond the buildings. And sky, which today was slightly overcast, a pearl-gray illuminated by the sun trying to break through.

"Where's the bus headed?" he asked, again keeping it light.

"Santa Barbara. Mom wants me to come up."

"Good."

He felt his posture relaxing. Grace Coyle was one of the all-time great mothers, just what Carmen needed right now. An actual parent, instead of a coward who used the smokescreen of looking out for her to cover the fact that he was too chicken to declare himself.

"Yeah, she has some kind of emergency with her hedges." Carmen gave a little chuckle. "Or so she says. I think Shannon called her and told her what happened on Monday and mom wants to see for herself that I'm all right." She sighed. "And you know what? It sounds nice, to get away, take a walk in the woods up there. Even though I guess I'm running away."

"From what?"

"You know. The job search. Hey, maybe I'll look for something up there, in the Santa Barbara area."

"Are you thinking of moving?" He said it offhandedly enough, but something inside seized up at the thought. *No.* No way Carmen could leave L.A. Leave him. Not okay.

"Probably not," she said. "I don't know. I didn't get

much sleep last night. Look—here's my bus. We'll talk later, okay?"

"Sure." And then she was gone.

He hung up the phone, a troubled frown forming between his brows. He'd never known Carmen to be this depressed, this lost and sad and defeated. But she was. And, like clockwork, that ache in the area of his heart was back.

The nursery might have been midsize, but it was chock full of healthy green plants, shrubs, trees and flowers. Carmen felt downright jubilant as she sniffed the air. Yes! Mulch and freshly watered grass, a tang of fertilizer, mist from the low-hanging fog that almost always filled the skies above Santa Barbara—all of it combined to make a simply heavenly smell, her own version of the perfect perfume, courtesy of Mother Nature. It cleaned out her pores and her troubled head, made everything okay again.

"I think several of these will do," she told her mother happily, adding some tulip and narcissus bulbs to her cart that was already overflowing with other bulbs and individual plants in temporary cardboard pots.

Grace Coyle smiled warmly at her daughter, the fine lines radiating from her gray eyes the only indication that she was no longer in her forties and was already solidly in her fifties. "I knew you'd find the right thing. You've always been so gifted, my green-thumb girl," she said, just a hint of her Boston origins still in evidence.

She put an arm around Carmen's waist and gave her cheek a kiss, having to reach up to do it. Her mother was short and compact, attractively rounded, like Shannon.

Carmen and her baby brother, Shane, took after Dad, as they were tall and long-limbed.

"I'm so glad you came up," Grace added.

"And I'm amazed. You actually *did* need me to do some plant doctoring—those Japanese weevils have just about devastated the hedge."

"Of course I needed you. I had been putting off asking you to spend some time in my garden, but then when I heard what happened the other day, I thought you might welcome the change of scenery."

"Oh, Mom, you know me way too well."

"I sincerely hope I do, after all these years."

Carmen chose a few verbena shrubs to set off the dark-pink color of the bougainvillea. "It's funny, though," she said, eyeing an orange-flowered plant she'd never heard of and deciding against it, "how well you do know me, considering how different we are. Like night and day."

"Mothers and daughters often are."

"You and Shannon are so much alike it's scary."

Grace frowned. "But I don't love her any more than I do you."

"Well, I know that," Carmen said with a grin. "I'm not talking about *that*." Perhaps one or two salvia superba, she thought, for a little change of pace in that shaded corner of the patio. "I'm so different from all of you," she said offhandedly. "You and Shan and Shane, and even Dad. I used to think I was a Martian, you know, someone from another planet who had been dumped on this poor, unsuspecting family." She chuckled. "Then later, I got that that was just a fantasy and decided I must have been adopted. You know, left at the doorstep and you and Dad took me in out of the kindness of your hearts."

"Oh, Carmen."

The distress she heard in her mother's voice drew her attention away from the plants she was considering. "Mom, I'm sorry," she said, instantly contrite. "This was back when I was a kid. Not a biggie now, trust me."

Grace's face resumed its usual good-humored expression as she nodded. "Actually, being adopted *is* a fairly common childhood fantasy. I see it in my clients all the time." Grace had her master's in child psychology and had a thriving practice.

"Yeah, I know I'm not unique." Carmen propped a hip against her cart, thought about it for a moment. "But you know I'm right. I mean, I just didn't…fit in. You, all of you, you worried about me because I was so different, remember? You all just *loved* school, and science and math problems were fun. And you sat around reading all the time—newspapers and these thick journals with tiny print. I read fiction and made weird clothing for my dolls and had trouble sitting still." She smiled, squeezed her mother's hand. "This is not about poor Carmen, I promise. I'm not feeling sorry for myself. It's just that I'm, well, I'm *different,* admit it."

Grace gazed at her for a long moment before assuming what Carmen had always thought of as her professor face. "But you're using the obvious markers—mathematical aptitude, school grades—that are only two of the countless traits we inherit from our families. You're very bright, extremely intuitive. You're just not a scholar. There are worse things in life."

Carmen raised a brow. "Says the woman with two master's degrees."

"The same woman whose garden—" she pronounced it gah-den "—always looks like the 'before' in a 'before and after' home improvement ad."

Carmen waved it away. "All it needs is a little love and water."

"Says the woman who makes things bloom just by smiling at them." Grace raised an eyebrow. "See? I can't do that. In fact, I stink at that."

"I know. Remember when Dad used to come in from the backyard, shake his head and say, 'The black-thumb strikes again'?"

"Which used to get my dander up something fierce. Even though he was right."

"About so many things."

Both mother and daughter's eyes filled briefly, then they smiled bittersweet smiles at each other. It had been four years since Gerald Coyle's untimely death in a small plane crash, and the lack of his presence in all their lives was still felt deeply.

"Okay," Grace said, clapping her hands. "Enough digression. Back to making my garden bloom."

"Yes, ma'am."

The cart was overflowing as they headed for the car. Out in the parking lot, as they passed an old station wagon, a dog began to bark. It was a similar bark to Bonzo's and the sound made Carmen's heart pound.

Like *that,* the lovely sense of well-being was shattered. It came back to her, the thing she'd been able to forget since being in Santa Barbara for the past few hours. Last night's terror, the barking dog and the sound of garbage can lids clattering and running feet. In the warmth of Grace's love and gentle presence, among the earthy smells of a nursery, she'd managed to put the incident and its unsettling aftereffect away, but now it was back.

Someone had been trying to get into her house. A figure in black, Gidget had said. Carmen's imagination had made the leap to connecting that figure with the incident at Nordstrom.

Which, if she thought about it, didn't really make sense.

First of all, Monday's murder had nothing to do with her—she'd been the classic innocent bystander, that was all. Secondly, she lived in a high-crime neighborhood, where robberies were frequent. And, thirdly, didn't dressing in black make sense if you were robbing people at night?

Which brought to mind how lucky Carmen was that Gidget's dog barked at intruders. Lucky even that Gidget slept in the nearby alleyway and, in a funny way, watched over her. Amazing. A homeless woman, acting as her protector.

Protector.

There it was again, that word, Carmen thought as she loaded the plants carefully into the back of her mom's ancient station wagon. Yet one more protector for the screwup. JR and Mom and Dad and Shannon and Shane and Gidget. The list was endless. Step right up, ladies and gentlemen. Come take care of this poor, clueless girl who can't seem to get it together enough to take care of herself.

Hold it right there. Carmen shook her head to clear it. What in the world was she doing? Heavy self-pity was *so* not her style. The bright side, she always made herself look on the bright side. Which was…?

That she was alive. She was healthy. She was loved. She was young enough to make changes.

And she *adored* gardening. This afternoon, she would plant the flowers and shrubs she'd chosen for Grace, maybe take a walk in the woods that abutted the small abode-styled house Mom had moved to after Dad's death. Something positive, some next step, would come to her. She just knew it.

She turned around and gave her mother a kiss on the cheek.

"What was that for?" Grace said, gray eyes twinkling.

"Just because I love you." Her mood having lightened considerably, Carmen hummed as she finished loading all kinds of lovely plants into her mother's car.

The intercom buzzed. JR, just back from the Venice storefront and eating a sandwich at his desk while catching up on his work, said absently, "Yes, Daisy?"

"There's a Detective Marshall on line four for you."

"Thanks." Curious as to why the detective would be calling him, JR punched in the button and the speakerphone. "Detective?"

"Mr. Ewing. How are you?"

"It's JR and I'm fine. What's up?"

"I've been trying to get hold of Ms. Coyle. I've left a couple of messages for her, but she hasn't gotten back to me."

"I'm sure she'll get back to you eventually."

"Yeah, well, I need her sooner than 'eventually.' Do you know where she is or how I can reach her? Does she have a cell phone?"

"Detective?" JR smiled. "Remember that you're talking to a lawyer."

"I remembered, trust me," Mac said dryly.

"And that means before I give you any information about Carmen, I want to be sure her best interests are being served."

"Fine. Okay, first of all, we've released the dead woman's identity and she wanted to know that. It's Margaret Davis. Peg for short. Her husband's on his way back to the States and the funeral is on Friday."

"Thanks. Anything else?"

"Yes. We're reinterviewing all the witnesses."

"All of them?"

The detective sighed the sigh of the world-weary. "Look, we know she didn't kill the woman, and as far as we know, she has no connection with the victim."

"But…?"

"Her name has…come up."

"Oh?"

He expelled an irritated breath. "Counselor, all I want to do is talk to her. Do you know where she is? Again, does she have a cell phone?"

Her name had "come up," JR thought. He could have asked in what context, but he was pretty sure he already knew. The police had had time to delve more deeply into the witnesses' backgrounds, including Carmen's, and learn about her association with Tio Schluter. JR's two years in the D.A.'s office had taught him that any hint, the merest sniff of law-breaking or association with lawbreakers, and she'd be placed right on the front burner. A Person of Interest. It was the way the cops worked and, ninety-five percent of the time, they were right to do so.

It was just that Carmen, his Carmen, belonged in that other five percent, and he would make sure the authorities knew it.

"Detective, I'll see if I can locate her and pass along your message."

"Will that be 'eventually' or 'sooner'?" he asked.

JR smiled. "We can only hope it's the latter. Goodbye."

Carmen ran her tongue over her mouth as she washed off a dinner plate before handing it to Grace, who was on drying duty. "You ought to franchise your spaghetti sauce, Mom, honest. It has to be the most delicious ever."

Grace laughed softly. "And you're feeling better, aren't you?"

Carmen handed her mother the clean plate and grinned at her. "What was your first clue?"

"The fact that you actually ate your dinner. I couldn't get you to take a bite at lunch and you completely avoided the cookies I brought out this afternoon. You and I are the exact opposite. When I'm troubled, I eat. When you're troubled, you lose your appetite."

The ringing wall phone made Grace reach for the receiver. "Hello?…JR. How nice to hear from you… Yes, she is." Smiling, she handed the phone to Carmen.

After wiping her hands, she took the phone. "Hi, JR," she said, feeling uncharacteristically shy.

Their conversation this morning had been an awkward one, and she'd thought about him intermittently for much of the day, especially in light of what Shannon had said about his feelings for her. Was it possible her sister was right? Or was it her older sibling's own love-life-deprived state that made her see hearts and flowers where none existed?

"I thought you'd want to know," JR said. "The shooting victim's name is Margaret Davis, Peg for short. The funeral is the day after tomorrow."

In a flash, the pictures in her head came back. The woman lying on the floor of the dressing room, blood pumping out of her. Carmen had to swallow before saying, "I want to be there. I'll get a bus out tomorrow."

"I have a deposition in Ventura at ten a.m. tomorrow, so why don't I swing by in the afternoon and pick you up?"

"It's out of your way, JR. Really, I'm fine on the bus."

Her mother, hands deep in soapy water, glanced over at her with a questioning look in her eyes. Carmen put her hand over the mouthpiece. "He'll be in Ventura tomorrow and wants to drive me back."

"And your problem with that is…?"

At the same time she heard JR say, "Carmen, I'm practically there. I'm not going out of my way, I promise."

She was cutting off her nose to spite her face, as the expression went. A pretty silly expression, if you thought about it, all those discarded noses. "Well, okay. Yes."

The problem wasn't just that JR would be going out of his way—and whether he said it or not, he was—but that Carmen didn't, or part of her didn't, want to go home. The thought of walking in the door of her little house gave her the willies. That sudden, shattering noise last night. The fleeing person in black that Gidget had seen.

Which, if she stopped to think about it, might or might not have been the truth, given Gidget's propensity for fantasy….

But she had to go home eventually, right? She needed

to get on with Phase Two of her life—the meaningful employment/career search. Mom had suggested she get some vocational aptitude testing. Not a bad idea. And in the meantime, she could probably get a job at a different nursery from the one she'd worked at before. It was the one thing she shone at, wasn't it? And sure, it might not be big money, but maybe she could advance.

Remembering the pep talk she'd given herself earlier in the day, she nodded. There was a place for her. Somewhere. There just *had* to be.

During the two-hour ride back from Santa Barbara the next day, Carmen and JR automatically resumed their old, easy, relaxed way of interrelating, which was a huge relief to Carmen. He spoke about an interesting new invention one of his clients was working on and Carmen recounted some of Mom's career suggestions. She waxed enthusiastically about all the new colors in Grace's garden and he got her laughing at a new lawyer joke.

And as the ride went on, Carmen decided Shannon was wrong. JR wasn't in love with her; no, he simply adored her the way she adored him. They had this long, shared history, hours of talking and laughing, and just, well, just being friends.

Then why, she had to wonder, did she keep taking peeks at his profile as he drove? Such a nice profile. A strong profile, in fact. And his mouth. It was a very sensual mouth. Why had she never really noticed his mouth?

Because he was JR, she reminded herself. Practically her *brother,* they'd known each other so long. Although *not* her brother, in actual fact, which was the good news. Especially considering the sexy parts of the dream.

The minute they got back to her place, JR headed for her kitchen sink and poured himself a glass of water. The ever-changing Southern California weather had turned hot. Eighty degrees in November, even at 5:00 p.m. He'd long ago removed his suit jacket, loosened his tie and rolled up the sleeves of his shirt, and now Carmen watched him as he took a drink. Such nice forearms. Long muscles, a fine sprinkling of light hair. Large hands. Had she ever really noticed his hands? Long fingers. Sturdy.

What would it be like to touch him, to feel those long, sturdy fingers on her skin?

Stop it.

She told herself to remember way back when he'd first come into her life over twenty years ago. The sunken chest, the skinny arms. The bottle-thick glasses. Even though she'd been a year younger, she'd gotten her growth spurts before he did, and he'd been deeply unhappy about it.

He'd since caught up, and had several inches on her now. Yup, JR was fully grown and quite a man, at that. A sort of…intellectual hunk. Emphasis on the hunk. Yum.

No!

JR was her friend, for heaven's sake. She'd seen him through most of his love life, as he had seen her through hers. He'd had three or four semiserious relationships. They'd tried double-dating, but it never worked; her guys were more brawn than brain, and he always went for that classy, *Wall Street Journal*-subscriber type. The not-Carmen type.

"Carm?"

"Huh?"

He was finished with his water and was gazing at her with amused affection. "You're away in your head somewhere."

"Oh, was I? Not a great neighborhood to visit, trust me."

Mentally chastising herself, she walked into the living area and checked it out. All appeared to be as usual—clean, but cluttered. Nothing out of place, except for the stuff that was always out of place *chez* Carmen. Which meant no one had broken in. Whew.

Should she tell JR what had happened? He would worry. And hadn't she discounted it as anything important? Noises in the night, that was all. Big whoop. No, she decided. Not worth it.

"Well," JR said, "I'd better take off."

"Oh, I hoped you'd stay."

"I can't. Sorry. But I'll pick you up for the funeral tomorrow, nine o'clock. Okay?"

"Why can't you stay?"

He offered a one-shoulder shrug and looked uncomfortable. "I'm busy."

"Got a hot date?" she teased.

"A date, yeah. Whether it's hot or not, I don't know."

"Oh." Her stomach plummeted to the floor. "Anyone I should know about?" she asked lightly.

"I just met her. A lawyer from another firm in our building."

"Oh, well, good. Have a great time." She turned away, astonished at the sick feeling of jealousy, even *hurt,* that she felt. This was nuts, totally and completely wacko. Having all these emotions about JR!

"Carm?" she heard him say behind her.

She kept walking toward the door. "Yes?"

"Remember what I told you. Don't talk to Mac unless I'm with you."

"Got it." At the door, smile firmly in place, she turned around to face him. JR stood right there, close, and smelling wonderfully of male sweat and aftershave. "Go," she said lightly. "Get gorgeous for your date."

And then she did the silliest thing. She reached up and stroked her knuckles along his jawline, just beginning to get bristly, so many hours after his early-morning shave. And, even sillier, she stood on her tiptoes and kissed him. Lightly, just a friendly little goodbye-between-friends peck on the mouth.

Which didn't end right away. No, there were sensations to record first: the surprising softness of his mouth, the firm, smooth skin of his lips, still moist after his glass of water. She had the craziest urge to run her tongue over those lips, sip from the same water. She held back...but, still, she lingered, just for a moment or two. She'd kissed him before, of course, but as an afterthought. This was no longer an afterthought.

JR's immediate reaction, Carmen couldn't help noticing, was to stiffen, as though taken aback. But that didn't last long, because he made a noise in the back of his throat, put his arms around her, drew her close and deepened the kiss, slanting his mouth to take more of her. As he did, the shock of discovery that went through her system made her gasp. It was the smallest, most sensual touch of his tongue that caused her heart to leap into her throat, her nipples to harden, and set up an instant throbbing between her legs. *Uh-oh*.

Cheeks flushed with embarrassment, she took a step

back, putting distance between them. "Go," she said with a little laugh, averting her eyes.

"Carm?"

It wasn't easy but she made herself look at him. The expression on his face was priceless. Turned on, oh yeah. And shocked, too. Totally, completely, thoroughly thrown for a loop. JR was never thrown for a loop.

"Carm?" he said again, his voice gravelly, his gaze pinning her with both wonder and sexual intensity. "You kissed me."

"Hey, I've been doing that all our lives. Go, now."

"But—"

She grabbed the doorknob, yanked the door open and stepped aside. "Go," she said, more firmly now.

He stared at her, obviously trying to get a grip on what was happening.

"Go, JR," she said again, more softly now. "Please."

After locking gazes with her for another few moments, finally, he gave a quick nod and walked out the door.

She closed it behind him. Then and only then did she raise trembling fingers to her mouth. To touch the very place his lips had touched. "Whew," she said aloud, stroking her fingertips over the heated skin of her lips. Closing her eyes, she leaned against the closed door and drifted into some kind of trance.

She had no idea how long it lasted, but the sound of knocking brought her back to reality. Had JR forgotten something? Or had he come back for more of what he'd tasted?

Smiling to herself, Carmen opened the door to see Detective Marshall standing on the porch. A fine layer of perspiration covered his brown face, his tie was askew and he wore another droopy sports jacket, dull green this time. "Ms. Coyle. May I come in?"

"I'm not supposed to talk to you. JR said."

"Okay then," he said easily. "How about if I talk to you? You don't have to say a thing."

She knew she shouldn't let him in, that she'd given her word. But she was curious about this case, felt a deep, personal need to know more. And—maybe she was a fool—but she trusted Mac. Probably shouldn't, but she did.

She stood aside and he entered the room, surveying it as he did, then nodding. "Nice," he said appreciatively.

"Really?"

"Yeah. It looks cozy. You know, comfortable. Colorful. I like colors."

She loved her little nest, so his comment pleased her, and she found herself relaxing just a bit more. "Can I get you something? A soda?"

"Nothing, thanks. May I sit?" He indicated the wooden chair adjacent to her overstuffed sofa.

"Sure." She moved over to the couch, sat and curled her legs under her. "What is it you want to say to me and that I don't have to answer?"

"Just that the other day…I should have asked you more questions."

"I told you all I remember."

"Did you?"

"Yes." She had nothing to hide, she reminded herself. Nothing.

"I checked up on you," Detective Marshall said.

"Checked up on me?" She already knew he had, of course; JR had told her.

"We're still no further along on the Nordstrom case. When we come up against a brick wall like this, we do background checks of the witnesses. And I got a report from Culver City P.D. about you. Well, about Phillip Tioka Schluter, dope dealer and small-time grifter. You're his girlfriend."

"Was."

He shrugged. "Okay, was."

He gazed at her, as though expecting her to expand on her answer, to say something. Something incriminating? What else? So he'd lied—gee, what a surprise! He *did* expect her to talk to him. She sighed. She was an idiot, Carmen told herself ruefully as she got up and walked toward the door. "I think you'd better leave."

"Why? We're just having a little chat." He remained seated.

She shook her head, then crossed her arms over her chest. He was doing cop tricks—she'd seen them on TV plenty of times. "If you read the report from Culver City, you know I had nothing to do with Tio and his illegal activities. Besides, what does that have to do with the murder?"

He spread his hands. "Those of us in law enforcement operate on a 'where there's smoke, there's usually fire' kind of theory."

Again, she shook her head. "Not this time. No smoke, no fire. Sorry. I really do think you'd better leave now."

He went back to staring again, and most definitely *not* leaving. And yeah, it was having an effect, starting to make her nervous, which was precisely his intention.

Frustrated, she moved away from her visitor and

found herself pacing, something she always did when she couldn't keep still. "Look, my only connection to what happened at Nordstrom is that I tried to save someone's life and I failed." Her gaze roamed the room restlessly, taking in a small stuffed elephant JR had bought her years ago that now rested on the fireplace mantel. "It was a terrible day, the worst day of my life." A framed photo of her dad and mom and all three kids from way back hung on the wall and briefly drew her attention. "But I was a witness, that's all. There's no other connection." Her gaze hopped around some more, finally coming to settle on a shopping bag she'd shoved into a corner.

Her brow puckered for a minute. A shopping bag. A *Nordstrom* shopping bag....

She snapped her fingers. There it was, that thing she'd forgotten the last time Mac had interviewed her. "The sandals," she said out loud.

"Excuse me?"

She whirled around to face him. "I'm sure it's nothing but the other day you asked me if there was anything else I could add to my statement, and there was, but I couldn't think of what, but now I remember. The woman, Mrs. Davis? She was wearing the same sandals as I was."

She rushed over to the shopping bag and pulled out the box, opened it up, took out the sandals and brought them over to Mac. "Look familiar?"

Now the detective stood, grabbed the shoes and frowned at them. "They were on her feet. Covered with blood."

"Yes."

"How did you get them?" He was confused; it was obvious.

"No, no, they're mine. There are two pairs. She and I bought the same shoes. At separate times, of course. They were on sale," she added for no particular reason.

"But I didn't see you wearing them that day. I would have remembered."

"That's because after I bought them I wore them up to the dressing rooms, but I kicked them off to try on some suits. You know, to pretend I was wearing heels? They were a distraction—all the colors and that huge flower. You see? And then, after the blood…I mean, after poor Mrs. Davis was shot and I cleaned up, I put them back in the box and wore the rubber thongs I'd had on earlier. It's probably nothing important, but—"

The look on his face stopped her nervous monologue cold and told her that she was wrong. Very wrong. What she'd just told him *was* important. Extremely important.

As the full significance of what she had just said hit her, Carmen gasped. Her hand flew to her mouth. "Oh, my God."

Stern-faced, Mac nodded slowly. "Yeah. If the shooter came into the dressing rooms and identified the victim by what shoes she was wearing, it's possible, more than possible, that you were the intended target."

Chapter 4

JR's cell phone rang. After looking at the readout, he picked it right up. "Carm?"

"Hey," she said shakily.

"What's wrong?" he asked, instantly alarmed. He knew her too well.

"I'm sorry about your date, but that detective, Mac? He's here."

"Put him on. Now."

"Marshall here."

In his car, JR pulled over to the side of the road; he could usually talk on his cell and drive at the same time, but the added element of fear—which he'd heard in Carmen's voice and which he was now feeling himself—was too much. "You weren't about to talk to Ms. Coyle without me present, were you?"

"Don't give me lawyer b.s.," the detective snapped. "This is pretty serious."

"What's happened?"

"Nothing much. If you ignore the fact that I think your girlfriend's life is in danger."

"She's not my girlfriend," he snapped back at the detective, then felt pretty stupid for responding to that part of the sentence instead of the important part. "And what are you talking about? No, don't bother, I'm ten minutes away. Put Carmen back on the phone." When she was on the line, he said, "Nothing. Not a word to him. Okay? I'll be right there."

He broke a law or two getting back to her place, then spewed several colorful curses during the traditional Venice parking-space hunt. When Mac opened the door of Carmen's little house eight minutes later, Carmen was fussing with some plants in the corner.

She looked up when he came through the door and gave him a poor imitation of a smile. "Hi." Her face was pale, her eyes huge.

He looked from Mac to Carmen and back again. "Fill me in."

The three of them sat around Carmen's small corner breakfast table. Within two minutes he had the complete picture and he didn't like it. In fact, it terrified him.

But he was a lawyer and he thought like a lawyer, which meant he tried not to jump to conclusions.

He directed his comments to Mac. "Okay, we have several choice theories here. Let's go with the first, that Peg Davis was the target and, for the present, you can't find any obvious reason for it."

"We're still digging, but she seems clean as a whistle."

"What about a random act?"

"Not likely," the detective said with a shrug, "but you can't ever rule that out."

"Okay, so that's two explanations. A hit, for reason or reasons unknown, on Peg Davis. Or a random act of violence against innocent bystander Peg Davis. Some gang initiation, maybe."

"Maybe."

He took in a breath and expelled it before saying, "Now, if Carmen was the intended victim instead of Mrs. Davis, we go back to an on-purpose hit or a random act again."

"Not liking the whole random-act thing, Counselor," Mac said.

"Why?"

"It doesn't have the usual earmarks—word on the street of someone taking credit afterward, some schizophrenic on the loose, making threats, some sort of sloppiness or screwup because the shooter's a nutcase. No, this was clean and professional. The gun—which was reported stolen three months ago, by the way—was left near the scene, no fingerprints. No way to ID the shooter. My gut is it was a hit, and my gut's been serving me pretty well for thirty years on the force."

"And you're thinking Carmen's association with Schluter has something to do with it?"

"Best guess, yeah. Remember, there aren't always logical reasons for some acts of violence. It could be payback for something he'd done to someone else," he said grimly. "Or Schluter himself thinks she knows something. Or seven other theories. There has to be more than she's telling us."

Carmen had been following the two men and their exchange, feeling just a bit like the ball being batted back and forth between two Ping-Pong paddles. "Hello? I'm here," she announced, "right at this very table. And I don't enjoy being discussed as though I were on another continent."

Both heads whipped around to face her. JR looked surprised, then rueful. "Sorry," he said. The detective said nothing.

"Both of you, please," she said. "Listen to me. You're on the wrong track."

"Humor me," Mac said. "Let's go over your association with Schluter one more time."

She heaved a huge sigh. Whatever, she thought, and again, she related the facts: Tio had told her he'd sold a house back in Philadelphia, that he was on the west coast because he had some screenplay ideas and wanted to develop them. Sure, he'd spent a lot of time at the Venice basketball hoops, playing with some of the regulars there, and quite a bit of time lying on the beach getting a tan—thinking, he'd told her, creating, working on ideas. The creative process. And yeah, sure, he'd get phone calls and go out late at night, but she'd figured it was his business, that he was making friends with industry people who went clubbing in the area, and he never got high or even had too much to drink in her presence, for sure, so she'd never connected him with anything other than what he'd told her. Just one more pilgrim to the Mecca of movie-making, trying to strike it rich.

"You see? Tio came and went on his own," she explained earnestly. "Told me nothing. Left nothing with me. Trust me on that, please."

She looked from Mac to JR. Their expressions let her know that they were *tolerating* her. She hated when men looked at women that way. In her gut, she was absolutely *positive* that her association with Tio had nothing to do with the recent murder, but somehow, she was not getting through.

"Fine," she said, throwing her hands up in the air. "Search the place if you want to. I give you permission."

"No, she doesn't," JR said. "Not without a warrant."

Thoroughly exasperated, she pushed her chair back, stood and began to pace. "There's nothing here. You know I don't do dope. After Tio took off and I found out what kind of a scumbag he was, I scoured the place to see if he left any of that behind. There's no paraphernalia, no Baggies, no pipes, no money, nothing."

At that moment, Mac's cell phone rang. "Excuse me," he said, and went into Carmen's small kitchen, where they heard him mumbling without being able to understand what he was saying.

Hands on hips, Carmen faced JR, who was still seated. "For sure, Tio didn't murder that woman. I mean, he wasn't the shooter. For one thing, he's much taller…and, well, bulkier, than the person I saw. And the thought of him hiring someone to shoot me? Well, whatever he is, he's not a cold-blooded murderer. I'm telling you, JR, this is not about Tio. It's not about me. It *has* to be about Mrs. Davis. Poor Mrs. Davis."

Every time she thought about the murder victim, the sadness came back, and this time was no different. That sense of desolation, the lump in her throat, the threatening tears. It might have been an unseasonably warm

November day, but she was chilled, so she wrapped her arms around her waist for protection.

JR rose quickly from his chair and faced her, gripping her upper arms, steadying her. "Carm. It's okay."

She gazed at him through moist eyes. "It's only a theory, you said, about me being the target. Just one of many."

"Yes, but it has to be considered. We have no choice."

Oh, God. She wanted so badly to be comforted by him.

She was the one who had taught JR to hug way back in prehormonal development days. She was the one who had introduced him to a whole world of affectionate touches, friendly back rubs, warm, physical, comfortable connectedness. He'd learned the lesson well, had become a *superior* hugger, and over the years she'd come to depend on his arms around her, the clean smell of him, the warmth of his embrace, the knowledge that he was always there.

But…hadn't JR told her not to need him so much, and hadn't she agreed that it was time?

And hadn't Shannon told her JR was in love with her, and didn't that put a whole new wrinkle in the once easy physical relationship between them? Hugs were out now, weren't they?

Shouldn't they be?

Oh, how she longed for the clock to be turned back to a week ago, before JR had given her a talking-to, before the murder, before hearing what Shannon had to say. She wanted him to hug her again with no worries about subtext. She wanted her life back.

Her life. Was someone trying to end her life? Out of nowhere, a huge sob rose in her throat.

"Carm?" JR's grip tightened on her arms.

No, she told herself, fighting her body's hysteria with every fiber of her being. It wasn't true. It couldn't be true. "I don't believe that my life is in danger."

JR stared at Carmen. He wanted to shake her until her teeth rattled. She was in such denial. Yes, it was one of the ways Carmen had always dealt with unpleasantness, by pushing anything she didn't want to face so far away that it barely affected her.

But not now. This threat to her life couldn't be ignored.

"Listen to me," he began, determined to get through, but he was interrupted by a knocking on her front door.

He probably overreacted, but then so did Mac, who came barreling out of the kitchen; together they rushed to the door and stood on either side of it as though standing guard at the palace gates. Carmen walked over and peered anxiously out of the curtained window.

"It's okay, it's only Gidget." She pulled open the door and said, "Hi, come on in."

But when the white-haired woman saw all three of her greeters, she got spooked, backed away and was on the verge of running off.

"It's okay, Gidget." Carmen smiled gently. "These are friends. You've met JR. Remember? And this is Mac."

Eyes narrowed in suspicion, the older woman looked from one man to the other and stayed right where she was. "I just wanted to check up on you, is all. Haven't seen you since the other night. Wanted to make sure you were safe."

"That's so sweet. I'm fine."

"You sure? Bonzo was pretty freaked."

"I'm fine," Carmen said again. "Sure I can't get you something? A glass of water? What about a cookie?"

"I'm good." The homeless woman offered a conspiratorial smile, one that revealed the lack of several teeth. "Found a box of unopened Oreos." She shook her head as she walked away, muttering, "The stuff people throw out. It's a crime."

After Carmen closed the door, JR looked at her and said, "What was that all about?" closely followed by Mac's "What about the other night?"

She walked away from them, raking her fingers through her hair. "I'm not sure," she answered. "It's all kind of a blur." She turned around, faced them, not at all happy, it was obvious. "What's today?"

"Thursday," both men answered, then looked at each other before transferring their attention back to Carmen.

"Okay then, Tuesday night I think someone tried to break in here. While I was sleeping. But I could be wrong. I really don't know. Gidget gets a little spacey sometimes. There was a noise in the alleyway, that's all."

JR's patience was growing thin. "You didn't tell me."

Carmen stuck her chin out. "I didn't think there was anything *to* tell. Whoever it was ran away. Gidget's dog barked."

"Gidget's the lady at the door just now?" Mac asked, his notebook out, scribbling away.

She nodded. "My neighbor."

"She's not really a neighbor," JR explained. "A homeless woman who sleeps in a huge carton in the alleyway. Carmen's kind of befriended her. Feeds her sometimes."

Mac nodded. Hearing about a homeless person wasn't news to him, not in the Santa Monica/Venice area, which a local radio satirist had pegged The Home of the Homeless. "Give me details. What happened?"

"I was sleeping and I woke up. There was some noise, garbage cans being turned over, that kind of thing."

"Okay, nothing unusual so far," Mac conceded.

"That's what I thought," Carmen agreed.

But she was holding back. "There's more," JR said. "I know you."

"Yes, there is." She straightened her shoulders, faced him. "Gidget saw a figure. In black. Wearing a baseball cap."

"Did you report it?" Mac again.

"No."

"Anything happen since then?"

"I wouldn't know." Again, she raked her fingers through her hair. "Yesterday morning I went up to Santa Barbara to be with my mother and I just got back. JR drove me."

JR looked at Mac. "I don't like this."

"Neither do I," Mac agreed.

"Can we get her some protection?"

"Probably not. I just asked my captain to issue an APB for Schluter, but until we find him, we're only working on a theory—we have no evidence, no proof of anything."

Boy, was Carmen getting sick of this! Sick of being discussed like she was some helpless victim, sick of all the testosterone in the room, all the advice, all the orders. She let her irritation turn into anger—not big-time anger, but enough to burn off the fear. She glared at them both.

"Listen to me. You have no way of knowing if the noise in the alleyway was in any way connected to what happened on Monday. No way at all. Get it through your heads. I may be a lot of things—disorganized, forgetful, even unreliable—but I know what I know. There is absolutely no reason on earth that I can think of for anyone to want me dead."

"But you don't know that for sure," JR said.

"But that could go for anyone. I mean, you or Mac or anyone! You can't live your life like there's some huge...*thing* you have no idea about, just waiting to get you. I'm not going to live my life like that. In fear and terror. I refuse, I absolutely refuse to start acting like a poor little paranoid victim."

She held her head up and glared at Mac, then at JR. "Look, both of you, go. I'm tired. I want to get some rest. Please, leave." She walked over to the door, pulled it open and stepped aside.

"Are you nuts?" JR said in disbelief, striding toward her.

Mac was more circumspect. "Ms. Coyle," he began.

"It's Carmen, remember?"

"Fine. Carmen. I highly advise you to stay with a friend tonight, at least until we can get this straightened out."

"Thank you. I'll consider it."

"Carm," JR said, standing right in front of her, his arms fisted at his sides, "come to my place."

"No thanks. I'll be fine."

"No, you won't, and I'm not leaving." She saw a small muscle in his jaw working overtime; he was well and truly pissed off at her. Well, the feeling was mutual.

"Yes, you *are* leaving," she said, glaring at him. "Dammit, JR. You can't have it both ways. You give me the lecture from hell about how I need to stop asking other people to clean up my messes, and then every time I try to take care of myself, you're right there, ready to hop in and fix it. Give it up. Get a life. Go on your date. I'll take care of myself."

His initial reaction to her outburst was to look stunned. Then, mouth in a thin line, he nodded. "All right. Fine."

What she'd said and the way she'd said it might have surprised him but it had totally blown her away. Wow. She never stood up for herself that way. Never. To anyone. What had come out of her mouth sounded more like Shannon than her; Carmen usually backed away from confrontation, walked out on arguments.

Not today, though.

And even though she knew both men's concern for her echoed her own and was founded on—she had to admit—real possibilities, standing up for herself had felt great!

Except that she'd hurt JR, just a little, she could see, and she hated that.

But still, she knew she was right. If any action was needed, she would take it herself. Filled with a new-but-not-unwelcome sensation of having grown a spine, she said, politely but pointedly, "Goodbye, gentlemen."

Both of them walked out the door, but stopped on the other side of the threshold. JR looked at Mac. "Can't you do anything?"

"I was about to ask you the same thing myself."

Her heart melted, just a little, at the sight of two highly masculine, action-oriented types thrown for a complete loss. "Thanks for caring so much," she said, adding, "I mean it," before closing the door.

She went to the window and watched them leave. After that, a quick glance down the alleyway let her know that Gidget's shopping cart was gone, which meant she and Bonzo wouldn't be around to stand guard.

Facts were facts. Night was closing in and she lived alone in a high-crime area. There had been an attempt to break in to her house the other night. She might have drawn a line in the sand, but she wasn't an idiot. She walked over to the phone and punched in her sister's number. "Shannon? It's me. Want company tonight?"

There wasn't much of a turnout at the funeral chapel the next morning—twenty or so people, all crowded up front near the casket. JR and Carmen sat halfway up the aisle. Every so often he glanced over to see how she was holding up. Apart from the look of sad sympathy on her face, she seemed okay.

He was not.

Yesterday, after she'd ordered him and Mac out, he'd kept watch on her place and had been relieved when, within the hour, Shannon had come for her. He'd watched them drive off, hadn't seen another car following and had finally relaxed...for the moment. When, later on, Carmen had called and asked him to pick her up at Shannon's for the funeral, he'd acted appropriately surprised at her location.

But he'd canceled his date for that night. He'd only made it because he'd been determined to get past this *thing* he felt for Carmen, the thing that had nothing to do with their long friendship. Love? Lust? A possibly neurotic need to rescue her? All of the above?

Was any of it returned?

She'd kissed him. Yesterday afternoon, after their return from Santa Barbara and before the entire sandals revelation, she'd kissed him. And he'd kissed her back. It was not a "friend" kiss; no, there had been a spark. More than a spark, the beginning of a flame, a two-way flame.

But he didn't know what it meant—to Carmen. Didn't know what to do with it or about it.

JR didn't like feeling this way. It felt passive and he was not, by nature, a passive man. He liked himself. He was hard-working and responsible, self-confident. He could be easy-going, but only up to a point, and then he could turn cold, decisive. Firm.

Except when it came to Carmen, to getting past this thing he felt for her. One kiss and he was waiting to see what would happen next. One whiff of danger to her, and he was ready to quit his job, sell his condo and drag her to another continent, if it would ensure her safety. Getting over Carmen? Not on today's agenda, that was for sure.

And so they were here at Peg Davis's funeral in Torrance. Carmen had dressed in what was, for her, conservative clothing. A long, navy-blue skirt with a print of pale tulips, and several layers on top—an off-the-shoulder T-shirt with something loosely woven over it that hung to her waist, and a knitted shawl around her shoulders, crystals dangling from her ears. Eclectic odds and ends, as always, and they somehow wound up working well. Carmen's clothes were all soft; they moved with her, accented her innate sensuality. He wondered sometimes if she was aware of the effect she had on others. Stirred *his* loins, for sure, every time.

Her attention at the moment seemed to be focused on Peg Davis's husband's back, as he sat stiffly in his Marines uniform. All around him were relatives and friends, the women sobbing softly and dressed in black.

JR angled his head around. Sure enough, Mac was

still there, in the rear, his gaze scanning the room, a frown on his face. When JR made eye contact with him, he nodded, once, then went back to his vigil. A uniformed cop stood to the side of the rear door, so Carmen was safe, at least for now.

When the service was over, JR and Carmen rose together and watched the family filing out. After they'd paid their respects, he glanced around for Mac, but he was nowhere in sight.

Outside in the parking lot, he asked her if she wanted to go to the graveside, but she shook her head. "We don't really belong there."

"Okay, then, where to now? I cleared the morning."

"You didn't have to do that, JR." Her smile was sweet, letting him know she was glad he had.

"I wanted to."

"Thanks." She thought for a moment, then her face lit up. "You know where I'd love to go? The Venice boardwalk. That always cheers me up."

"I was hoping you'd choose someplace a little less public, Carm."

Her gaze narrowed. "Because you think I'm a target?"

"It's a possibility."

"Didn't we have this discussion yesterday? And didn't I tell you I can't live my life that way?"

"I'd hoped you'd changed your mind."

"I didn't." She sighed, gazed around her. "JR, I saw a woman die a few days ago. And we just came from her funeral. Life is too short. Way too short. I won't live it looking over my shoulder. If someone is out to get me—and until you give me proof, I still don't think they are—then being out in the open air, surrounded by people, feels as safe to me as anyplace else. I'm going to the boardwalk."

"Then so am I."

As they drove north, JR tried to tamp down his anxiety about Carmen's safety. He kept an eye on the rearview mirror. From what he could tell, he didn't think they were being followed, but being on the lookout for bad guys in cars wasn't his job. Was Mac still with them?

When they'd spoken outside Carmen's little house yesterday, the detective had said all they had at the moment was a theory, and theories didn't warrant police protection. But Mac had promised he'd do all he could, at least until they knew if they were on the right trail.

And JR had believed him. He'd met many officers of the law over the years, had heard numerous horror stories from other lawyers, but Mac seemed to have a little more heart and a little less need to clear cases, no matter the cost, than most.

Carmen needed protection, that much JR knew, whether she wanted it or not. Maybe he would hire a private firm to do that. Even if she protested. He would do it anyway.

The Venice boardwalk was actually a long, paved strip that ran parallel to the ocean for several miles. It was a mix of new, upscale, ocean-view homes and run-down brick apartments in need of repair, alongside modest restaurants, businesses and shops. A mélange of vendors were set up on the ocean side of the walk, selling original art and jewelry, hawking tarot card readings and massages. There were deep discounts on socks, T-shirts, sunglasses and bikinis; body piercing and tattoos were available.

The day was a gray, overcast one; summer was gone and with it, the tourists. Even so, a steady stream of people of all ethnicities and ages rode by on bicycles, strolled, jogged and inline skated. At the outdoor basketball courts, a few men shot hoops; nearby, several muscular specimens worked diligently on becoming more so.

And pouring out of each storefront and vendor's cart, there was music. As Carmen and JR walked along, the music changed every few seconds, like a radio set to Scan. Salsa, rap, reggae, folk, Kanye West to Ella Fitzgerald to Beethoven. Carmen, with her amazing ability to escape reality, bopped and hummed along with each new rhythm. She seemed happy to be here.

JR, on the other hand, couldn't help wondering if any of the faces they passed belonged to a killer.

"Hey, JR," Carmen said with a happy smile. "Race you to the water." Before her words registered, she'd slipped off her shoes and was running over the sand toward the shoreline.

He took one last look around the crowd before kicking off his loafers, peeling off his dress socks and taking off after her. Hell, what did he know? Maybe being on guard was a waste of time. Was he allowing the atmosphere of the past few days to get to him? The murder, the investigation, Mac's frowning face, the funeral—had it influenced his thinking?

What were the odds, knowing what he did about Carmen and her life, that someone was actually trying to kill her? Maybe there was some other explanation for this entire thing, one that had nothing to do with Carmen being in danger.

"Carmen," he shouted as he gained on her, "give it up. You can't win!"

He managed to pass her but stopped short at the water's edge; she ran partway into the surf, holding her skirt above the waves, dancing and laughing. "It's freezing! Come on in."

"If it's freezing, why would I want to?"

"Chicken!"

"And proud of it," he replied, smiling at the picture she made, at the way the wind whipped her hair and made her skirt billow around her knees. When she came out, shivering, he grabbed her hand and they jogged for a while in silence along the shoreline in the clear chill of an autumn afternoon, while sunlight danced on the water.

After a while, they slowed down. Carmen said, "That poor man."

"Who?"

"Her husband. Sergeant Davis. So stoic. I hope he breaks down soon."

"Men grieve differently from women. Or most of them do."

"Why do you think men don't cry more?"

"We're taught not to. Society frowns. Or maybe it's all physiological. We have a different hormonal structure." JR shrugged. "Lots of reasons."

"But it's such a relief to cry." She angled her head to face him. "You don't cry, do you?"

"Not since I was a kid and someone took my Batman action figure."

"Poor JR. Who would have done such a cruel thing?"

He chuckled. "Pretty much anyone back then. Remember?"

Oh, yes, Carmen remembered. Her nerdy, awkward, socially backward little friend, Stanton Fitzgerald Ewing. Such a big name for such a little guy. He'd asked to be called Stan, but she'd refused, insisting instead that he call himself JR, after the character on the TV show, *Dallas*. The TV JR was cocky, confident and ruthless; Carmen had hoped her new friend would be a little more like a JR and a little less like a Stanley. For whatever reason, the name had stuck.

She took in a huge breath of sea air and sighed happily. Next to the smell of mulch and fertilizer and newly watered roses, this was her favorite. Once again the ocean was doing its magic, relaxing her, helping her to forget. "Yes!" she said, letting go of JR's hand, flinging her arms out and dancing in a circle, "I love the smell of rotten fish in the morning!"

That got a laugh out of him, so she went on. "And tides fascinate me. They come from so far away, thousands of miles, all the way from Asia, along with the winds and stuff. Sometimes I think about a wave and its journey. You know, like it's a person? It has this life span. It begins as this little bitty ripple thing, way, way back, and then it grows and gathers strength, and then it hits the shore and then it's over." She snapped her fingers. "A life. Gone. Like that."

For a moment it hit her again, the wasted young life of Peg Davis, and she nearly got sad again, but JR—who could always read her—gave her a crooked smile. "Waves aren't human, Carm," he said lightly. "They aren't even animals."

"I know. I just think about it."

He reached out, grabbed her by the arms and pulled

her to him. "You think about a lot of things, don't you," he said, smiling into her eyes. "Such a busy mind."

"Such a silly mind," she said with a laugh, even though her mouth had suddenly gone dry, "filled with all kinds of silly things."

He was close, so close. Was he about to hug her? And would it be a friendship hug? Or was JR going to kiss her, the way she had kissed him yesterday? Were they about to start something? And did she want it to start?

Oh, boy, talk about confusing.

Dancing away from him, she glanced around, hoping to find some distraction. "Oh, look," she said, bending over to pick up something shiny—a shell? An earring?—lying half-buried in the sand.

The next few seconds happened in a flash, too quickly for her brain to register details.

First she heard what sounded like a car backfiring, followed a fraction of a second later by a *whiz-z-z-z*ing sound above her head. Without thinking she began to straighten up, but was tackled by JR, and not gently.

"Hey!" she said, then didn't get a chance to say or think much of anything else as she heard another backfiring car—no, no, not a car, something in her mind yelled at her, a bullet! More *whiz-z-z*ing sounds. And JR was doing something weird—covering her body with his and rolling along the sand, over and over, like children tumbling down a snow-covered hill in the middle of winter. Only there was no hill. Or snow. They were on level ground, on the sand by the ocean.

She heard a man shouting and a woman's high-pitched scream. And finally, JR stopped making her roll over and over, coming to rest partly in the water. The ocean was freezing and she couldn't stop shaking. JR lay on top of her like a huge, immovable lump.

"JR?" she said, but he didn't answer. "Hey, get off of me."

JR still wasn't answering. Panicking, she pushed at him and managed to heave him aside so that he lay next to her, farther submerged in the water.

Scrambling onto her knees, she stared at him. His eyes were closed. She didn't see any blood, not at this angle. She shook his shoulder. He didn't respond.

He lay there, half in and half out of the ocean.

Lifeless.

Chapter 5

There was noise. Too much noise. People shouting, gulls crying, waves crashing and someone, way too close, screaming his name.

His eyelids fluttered open to see that the screamer was Carmen; the look on her face made him wonder if he was dead and seeing her from the vantage point of his own coffin. Then as he became aware of excruciating pain in his left shoulder, he knew he was still alive, and that Carmen was on the verge of losing it.

"Hey!" he said in what he thought was a forceful voice, but it came out a croak.

It was, at least, enough to cut her off in midscream.

"JR?" The expression in her large brown eyes changed from alarm to one of relief. "Oh, JR! I thought you were dead."

"What happened?"

"We were shot! I mean, you were. I think. Were you? Are you hurt?"

"My shoulder." He tried to reach his right hand around to touch the place that was throbbing, but she pushed it away and examined his left shoulder.

"Your suit has this rip in it, and the shirt, too. And there's blood. Some. But not a lot. I mean, not like the other day."

"Good news." It came out a grunt. The shoulder ached like a son of a bitch now; once more he closed his eyes against the pain.

Someone came rushing up, and he heard a familiar voice say, "Medics are on the way."

"Mac?" he managed.

"Yeah, Counselor."

"Did you get him?"

A curse, followed by, "No. I was too far away."

"It's his shoulder," Carmen said.

JR felt fingers at the pulse point in his throat. "Pulse is faster than normal, but it's steady," Mac said.

"How did you get here so fast?" he heard Carmen ask.

"Been following you all morning."

"Did you at least see who shot at us?"

The detective muttered, "If I'd had backup, I would have nabbed his ass. Figure in black, like the other day. And he got away. Again."

JR forced himself to open his eyes. Two faces loomed over him, one weary and disgruntled, the other pale and scared. He ran his tongue around his dry mouth. He could hear sirens now; his shoulder felt like it was on fire. "Damn, that hurts," he said, trying to get up.

Carmen was holding tightly to his right hand; now she squeezed it in warning. "Don't you dare move."

"I'm pretty sure it's just my shoulder."

"Stay put, Counselor," Mac said. "The paramedics are here. They're running toward us with a stretcher."

"I really don't think I need—"

"Shut up," Carmen said, her eyes moist with unshed tears. "Just shut up! Damn you, JR. You saved my life."

He managed a crooked smile. "And all I get is a 'Damn you'?"

"You idiot. You could have been killed."

"But *you* weren't." Truly, that was all that was important—didn't she see that?

And then the paramedics were there, and he was caught up in being fussed over by pros. He closed his eyes again, but heard snatches of conversation.

"Left shoulder…" "No other injuries…" "Bullet still lodged…"

He must have passed out or been given drugs because next thing he knew he was on a gurney, being hustled along brightly lit corridors. "Carm?" he called out.

"I'm here," he heard from somewhere behind him, and then darkness enveloped him once more.

Later—minutes? hours? days?—he fought his way out of a deep sleep and opened his eyes. His brain was fuzzy but he was aware of several facts at the same time. His shoulder ached. He was stretched out on a hospital bed with a guardrail up on one side. The room was dimly lit. There was an IV needle inserted in the top of his left hand.

And a blond head lay on the side of the bed with no guardrail, near his knees. The head belonged to Carmen;

the rest of her body was slumped all the way over in a visitor's chair. She was sound asleep. The position looked extremely uncomfortable. When she woke up, she would probably have a hell of a backache.

When she woke up...

Like that, it all came back to him. The sound of gunshots, his desperate need to get Carmen away from those sounds. The way his heart had raced in panic, the way fear had gripped him like it never had before.

Carmen was definitely a target. Someone wanted her dead. And they'd nearly gotten their wish.

Questions screamed in his head. Who? What? Why?

The throbbing in his shoulder grew worse. He angled his head around just enough to see white bandages peeking out from under the hospital gown he wore. Most likely, he'd been operated on. He managed to reach over to the side table and retrieve his glasses, which he put on. His shoulder did not appreciate the movement. An involuntary hiss of pain escaped from between his lips.

At the sound, Carmen's eyes fluttered open. Yawning, she sat up, then winced.

"You'd better stretch it out," JR said with some effort.

"What?" She was groggy; she'd never been the instantly-awake type.

"Your back. You fell asleep funny."

As she twisted back and forth in her chair, he saw her try to focus on him, muttering, "Hey, who's the patient here?"

He waited, watched as she came slightly more to life, yawned once more, opened her eyes a little wider. And then, like that, she was awake, and she let loose with that full, joyous grin of hers, lighting up everything in the dismal hospital room, even causing his own pain to lessen.

"JR!" she said happily.

"That's my name."

Carmen had never been so glad to see someone, *anyone,* in her life. JR was up! He was alive! She leaped from her chair and came to the head of the bed, putting her hand on his forehead. It was cool. Whew. "How do you feel?"

"Like someone stuffed a towel in my brain."

"It's the meds."

"I need more of them," he said, then closed his eyes and grimaced.

She pushed the button for the nurse. "We'll get you as many as you need, poor baby. What else can I do for you?"

He blew out a couple of breaths before saying, "I also have to go to the bathroom. But I'm pretty sure you can't do that for me."

"Oh. Umm...I'm not sure you should get out of bed, JR."

But he was already sitting up, throwing the covers off with his good hand. He swung his legs over the side; the movement made him wince once again.

"It's your shoulder," she said, wincing with him. "They took a bullet out of your shoulder."

"No kidding," he said dryly.

"I mean, you have to wear a sling, otherwise it will hurt. That's what the doctor said."

"Ah. What time is it?"

"Nearly ten."

"In the morning?"

"No, it's still night. Friday night."

He shook his head, as though to clear it. "I need to call someone at my office, tell them I—"

"It's okay," she interrupted. "I talked to your secretary, Daisy."

"What did you tell her?"

"Well, I sort of thought it wouldn't be a good idea to mention that you'd been shot—they're pretty conservative over there, right? So I told her you got real sick, stomach something. Was that all right?"

He nodded. "Good thinking, Carm. Thanks."

She knew he was in horrible pain, but he did that guy-being-stoic thing. Holding his left arm to his chest, pantomiming a sling, he got up, then stood for a moment, as though making sure of his balance. He then walked around the end of the bed, used his right hand to grab the IV pole and made his way to the bathroom. His hospital gown tied in the back, and Carmen was unexpectedly treated to a view of the back of his long, bare legs. More to the point, through the gaps that opened and closed as he walked, she also got some tantalizing glimpses of his buttocks.

JR, she couldn't help observing, had a truly excellent butt, firm and muscled from all the years of running. Heat rose to her face, and she nearly said, "Award-winning buns, JR, and do you need some help in there?"

But she stopped herself. Too out of left field. Instead, she began to pace and tried really hard not to think about why she was here, in a hospital room. Why JR was here. Because when she thought about it, she started shaking, and if she kept shaking, she'd be no good to JR. *He* was the one who had to be the focus of attention now. He was the one who had saved her life.

Guilt, lots of it, washed over her. She hadn't listened to him and Mac. Sure they were mistaken, she'd been all "I'll do it myself." And her dearest friend in the world was the one who was paying.

The bathroom door opened. Face pinched with pain, JR made his way back toward the bed, still holding his left arm to his chest and hanging on to the IV pole for support. He sat down on the edge of the bed and gazed at her, his face deeply serious. "Carmen. Someone is trying to kill you."

Fear sliced through her again, but she sat next to him and tried for a smile. "You think?"

"You have to go away, hide. Have you talked to Mac?"

"Yes. You—we—were shot at from behind that hedge that surrounds the public restrooms. They've tried to find witnesses, but so far, nothing."

He shook his head. "Well, at least we know that theory number two is correct—Peg Davis's murder was an accident. You were the original target." Her alarm must have showed in her expression because he grimaced. "God, Carm, I'm sorry."

She waved it away, wishing her face didn't show everything she was thinking and feeling. "It's the truth, I know. It's just...I'm having trouble getting my brain around it."

The nurse—young, pretty and overweight—came bustling in. When she saw JR sitting on the edge of the bed, she said cheerfully, "I see you're up."

"He needs some more pain medicine," Carmen said.

"Actually, I'll take a prescription instead." JR stood. "Where are my clothes?"

The nurse wasn't happy. "I don't think your doctor

wants you to leave until the morning. We need to watch for infection."

"We can watch for infection at home." Pulling the IV pole again, he made his way over to the small corner closet.

"JR," Carmen said, following him. "You just had surgery. You're in pain. Please."

"I'll be leaving," he told the nurse. "Please get this needle out of me and bring whatever papers I need to sign."

She shook her head. "I'll get the doctor on call," she said, and scurried out of the room.

"JR," Carmen pleaded again. "Get back into bed." At times, he could be the most stubborn man! And this, obviously, was one of those times.

He shook his head firmly as he used his right hand to remove the bag containing his clothing from the closet. "I hate hospitals. Spent too much time in them as a child."

"You did?"

He nodded. "Asthma."

"When did you have asthma?"

"Off and on until puberty. I grew out of it."

"You never told me." Wordlessly, he took his clothing into the bathroom and closed the door. "JR?" Carmen called, ticked off at him for keeping this from her all these years. "Why didn't you tell me?"

"There were reasons."

"What reasons?"

He opened the door, stuck his head out. "I was already a pretty poor specimen, and I didn't want you to know yet one more thing about me that made me less, well, manly."

"Manly? You were a boy."

"Okay, then, what's the word for boy-y?"

Her whoop of laughter actually got a reluctant smile out of him. First one this evening. Then he closed the door again. "I'll be out as soon as I'm dressed."

This time she did say it. "Need any help?"

There was a really long moment before he replied, "Um, maybe. I'll let you know."

Again, too restless to sit, Carmen paced back and forth. She allowed herself a brief fantasy of helping JR dress, then put it away—too distracting—before wondering how she could have been such close friends with JR without knowing he'd had asthma. And wondering, too, about all the other stuff she didn't know about him, because, of course, there had to be other stuff.

She stopped. Frowned. So much—way too much—of their friendship had been one-sided, she realized. Carmen had always been the needy one. What about JR? Who, if anyone, had tended to *his* needs? Was this lopsidedness all her fault? Had her personal dramas preoccupied her to the extent that she ignored what was going on with JR? Or did he deserve some of the blame? Had he taken great pains to keep her from knowing when he suffered? They would have to talk about this sometime soon.

When he opened the bathroom door, he had on his suit pants and loafers, no socks. He'd managed to get the hospital gown off, as far as it would go, at least; the IV mechanism blocked full removal, so the cotton gown hung limply from his left forearm. His chest was bare, except for the network of bandages crisscrossing his left shoulder and underarm. He really did have a nice chest,

Carmen observed, with well-developed pecs and flat abs. He was lean, yes, but still, definitely a babe magnet.

She wondered, maybe for the umpteenth time in the past few days, why she'd never truly noticed that about him before. Had she been wearing blinders?

"I can't seem to find my shirt," he said, frowning.

"They had to cut it off you."

"Oh. Then I guess the hospital gown will have to do. Would you mind helping me get it back on?"

She stayed right where she was, at the foot of the bed, and crossed her arms. "You were shot, JR, and you're in a lot of pain. Why are you doing this? Let's get you some pain pills, let me help you back into bed."

"Nope. I want to go home. And you're coming home with me. No one can get in without a key. It's a secure building. You'll be safe there, for now."

"Of course I'm going home with you," she said, giving up on getting him to change his mind. "I'm going to take care of you."

"You don't have to take care of me," he muttered.

"Too bad," she said cheerfully. "Okay, now, if you insist on being a macho idiot, let's get this hospital thingie on."

As she busied herself helping JR back into the hospital gown, Carmen noted the broad muscles of his back, the warm, golden color of his skin. She ran her tongue over her mouth. She wanted to kiss his skin, to *taste* him.

Ohmygod. It was, finally, time to face it. She was *attracted* to JR! There were all kinds of sensual tinglings in her body at the thought of, well, of being with him. She was hot for him. *Hot* for JR!

Was it real, this attraction? It had popped up only recently, right? The day after the Nordstrom shooting? Maybe it was some kind of survivor reaction—she'd read about that in a magazine. People getting physical with each other right after their lives had been threatened. A kind of primal need to rejoice in being alive. Maybe it would go away when all this was over.

Which was a good thing. After all, JR was her friend. Her best friend.

Your best friend who's in love with you. She could almost hear Shannon whispering in her ear.

But, really, wasn't it kind of...odd? He was *so* not her type. And she was *so* not his. Still, at the moment, survivor mentality or not, the feelings were here and they were real and they were new.

Or maybe they were old, as old as their friendship.

"Carm," JR said, interrupting her train of thought. "Plan to stay with me, at my place, for as long as it takes."

She came around to face him, batting her eyelashes. "Why, Gaylord," she said in a broad, Southern-belle accent, "how forward you are."

"Are you listening to me, Carmen?" he said without smiling. "You're not going back to your place. Not until we find out what's going on."

His single-mindedness was beginning to annoy her. "Hey. Has anyone ever told you that you like to give orders just a little too much?"

"Okay, yeah, when I'm scared, yes, I get pushy. And I'm terrified. Not for me. For you, Carm." Suddenly, out of nowhere, JR's blue eyes filled. "You...mean so much to me." Two thick drops made their way down his cheeks.

She stared, openmouthed and struck dumb. JR, who never cried, was moved to tears. Because of her!

Unbearably moved herself at the sight, Carmen reached up to stroke his face. "Oh, JR, the feeling is *so* mutual. You mean the world to me." With her thumb, she gently wiped away one of the tears that had fallen down his cheek, then planted a gentle kiss on the damp spot.

He was mortified. He wanted to die.

In his youth, before he learned how to take care of himself, JR had been pushed around by bullies. Once in high school, the elastic on his bathing trunks had given way during a swim meet, and he'd had to back out of the pool with his hands over his privates. Another time, in college, during pledge week, his fraternity brothers had pinned a truly pornographic sign on his back without his knowledge, and he'd been unaware of it for a full half day, even though sniggering and outright belly laughter had followed him wherever he went. So JR was not unfamiliar with being humiliated.

But this was, without a doubt, bar none, the worst yet.

He turned away from Carmen, using his right hand to swipe at his suddenly damp cheeks. "Ignore me. It's the meds," he muttered. "I'm not usually this emotional."

"I won't tell the manly men club," she teased.

She was making light of it; at another time, he might, too. But at this moment, nothing would make that terror of being perceived as weak go away. Sure, a man could cry—in theory, at least—but not when he was trying to be strong, when he *had* to be strong. Not when the woman he loved needed him to be a rock-solid support.

He was saved from further self-flagellation by the

sudden, loud eruption of salsa music. "Oops," Carmen said. "Forgot to turn off my cell."

She went searching for her purse; after she found it, she went searching for her phone, buried somewhere in the chaos of purse contents. When she finally found it, she flipped it open. "Oh, yes, hi…. I see…. Yes, he's still here… I… Yes."

"Who is it?"

"Hold on." She put a hand over the mouthpiece. "It's Detective Marshall." Carmen went back to listening to Mac, nodding. "Okay, yes…. He was just saying the same thing. Both of you have an annoying tendency to bark orders at me." Closing her eyes, she sighed loudly. "No, he wants to go home…. Yes, I'm going with him…. Oh, right. Hold on." She directed the next bit to JR. "Your car. It's still in Venice where we parked it this morning."

"Actually, it probably isn't. Let me talk to him." When she handed him the phone, he said, "Mac?"

"How you doing, Counselor?"

"I've been better. Thanks for all you did today, by the way."

"Just doing my job."

"Thanks anyway," he said. "Listen, my car was probably towed. I was parked in one of those two-hours-only zones, and the parking police in that area are pretty vigilant."

"Yup, it was probably towed."

"Anything you can do about that?"

"I'll see. Meantime, if you're insisting on leaving, I'll be there in a half hour or so. I'll drive you both back to your place."

"You don't have to."

"It's ten p.m. I'm just getting off my shift. I'll be downstairs. After what you went through today, you deserve a police escort, don't you think?"

Between doctor's lectures, paperwork and getting the prescription filled, it was nearly midnight by the time Carmen and Mac got JR back to his place. At the door, Mac met her eyes. "My boss wants you down at headquarters for a chat."

"Why?" she asked. "I mean, I've told you all I know."

"Maybe, but there have been two shootings in public places and that's a major menace to society. So we interview you again, dig deeper this time, find out what we might be missing."

"Good idea," JR said. "I'll be there with her, of course."

Carmen slanted him a doubt-filled look. "You need to rest. I'll ask Shannon."

He ignored her. "Tomorrow morning, okay, Mac?"

"Fine. We'll be taping her statement. I want experts to hear it and determine if there's something we need to follow up on."

"What about protection?"

"I'm on it."

"Good."

They were doing it again, discussing her as though she wasn't in the room. Part of her was annoyed, but another part understood that men would be men, and the "protecting the womenfolk" segment of their brains was hardwired.

Her concern, at this moment, was getting JR to rest. She put a hand on his arm. "We'll be there in the morning, Mac," she said. "And thanks again for everything."

After she got JR settled into bed and gave him a pill, he announced he was starving. Thrilled to be able to do something, anything, for him, she went into the kitchen and whipped up some eggs and toast. By the time she brought them to him on a tray, he was sound asleep. So she sat in a chair by his bed, watched him sleep and ate them herself.

He woke up in the middle of the night, his mouth dry as sandpaper. He was halfway out of bed before searing pain reminded him he needed to favor his wounded side. He grit his teeth against the ache in his shoulder as he made his way out of the bedroom. Water. Pain pill. Food. In that order. He paused to glance into the living room, where Carmen lay asleep on his couch, dressed in a pair of his sweats, all curled up around a blissful Owl.

Lucky cat, JR thought, walking over to the couch. As though the feline had read his mind, he looked up at him through amber eyes, opened his mouth, yawned, then gave a small, satisfied "Mew."

"Don't rub it in," JR whispered, scratching the animal behind his ears. As he gazed again at Carmen's lovely face, all thoughts of getting a drink of water or food or a pill vanished.

The Carmen ache in his heart was back. He couldn't put it off any longer; he needed to tell her how he felt. Even if it wasn't returned—he'd deal with that when, and if, it happened. Truth-telling was important to JR; anything other than coming clean with her wasn't valuing himself and his standards.

Hold it. What was he thinking? Carmen was in danger. Their private lives, any romantic or sexual considerations, had to wait until they knew where the danger came from and how to defuse it.

Good intentions were admirable, but they didn't prevent him from being blindsided when he walked into the bathroom to get a pain pill and was greeted by the sight of her damp undies and bra hanging over the shower stall. They were pale peach and sheer and extremely feminine. Just looking at them, he felt himself grow hard as the proverbial rock.

JR might have decided to put the discussion of his and Carmen's relationship temporarily on hold, but his body hadn't gone along with the plan. Damn, he thought. His shoulder was killing him, the woman he loved was a target and he had a good, old-fashioned boner. Didn't get much more surreal than that.

At the West L.A. police station, this time they sat in an interview room, the kind with one-way mirrors, cameras and recording devices. And this time, it wasn't Mac conducting the investigation, but a detective Jackson Rutherford, who, Carmen decided instantly, could have gotten a callback on an audition for Tough Cop Number One. Short hair, the "I need a shave but so what?" look, buffed body, hard eyes, a mouth unfamiliar with smiling—Rutherford would always be the perennial bad cop in the bad cop/good cop game. If there were any warmth or compassion in the man, it sure wasn't there on his face.

He made her shiver, even though she knew she had nothing to feel guilty about, as he rattled off questions at her. She answered as best she could. JR interrupted a lot, slowed her down, slowed Rutherford down, which pissed him off, she could tell. The enmity between the two men had been obvious the moment they'd met, but remained just below the surface.

At one point, she glanced over at Mac. So far, the brown-skinned detective had stayed in the background, hadn't opened his mouth, let Rutherford do all the questioning. She wondered if he'd been ordered to step back, or what. She smiled at him; he didn't smile back, but she could have sworn he winked. Just a quick little flicker of an eyelid. It might have been her imagination, but it warmed her.

She answered question after question about Tio. Then the questions became more personal. About her life, her *entire* life. Her so-so grades, her spotty work history, the men in her past, losers, all of them. Maybe not as bad as Tio, but in the ballpark. How had she let her life get so far away from her?

It was when Rutherford insinuated—no, more than insinuated this time, suggested—that she was more involved in her ex's drug deals than it appeared on the surface, that JR scraped back his chair and stood. "That's it. Interview over."

"Pardon me?" Rutherford said with an arched eyebrow.

"You're getting perilously close to hinting that my client has broken the law in a serious way, and has somehow played a part in causing someone to come after her. That is not only unfair and patently untrue, it lets me know that you're fishing. You have two incidents, a murder and an attempted murder. Do your work, Detective. Don't start flinging accusations where there is no basis." He

walked over to the door, pushed it open and nodded to
Carmen. "Come on, Carmen, we're out of here."

"I'm not done yet," Rutherford said.

"*We* are," JR replied firmly.

Rutherford didn't stop them, couldn't, really, unless
he wanted to arrest her, and JR had explained that they
had no basis for doing so. As they walked away from
the interview room, Carmen took a look at his face. He
was still scowling, the muscles along his jawline working overtime.

"Hey," she said. "You may not be a D.A. anymore, but
you sure know your stuff. And you can quit acting now."

"It wasn't an act."

"Really? You seemed so pissed off, I thought it was
one of your lawyer maneuvers."

He muttered a word he rarely used in her presence.
"No, it was real. With the way Rutherford was talking to
you, I nearly grabbed him by the tie and knocked his head
off. Until I remembered that one arm was in a sling." He
shot her a look filled with self-disgust. "I couldn't detach,
the way a lawyer is supposed to. I couldn't keep my cool."

"Just like Tommy Spencer."

"Who?"

"In the park back when I was in the fourth grade. He
was teasing me and I was crying and you came running
up and pushed him, remember? And he was, like, thirty
pounds heavier than you and he pushed you back?"

His small chuckle was not amused. "Yeah, well,
that's childhood stuff and this is now."

Mac caught up to them as they were exiting the
police station. "I got a line on your car, Counselor.
Come on, I'll take you to the towing facility."

JR sat in the back of Mac's car during the trip. Carmen could see that, one, he was in a lot of pain but not complaining and, two, he was still unable to shake his anger. At Rutherford or at himself, she couldn't tell.

"Take a pain pill, JR. You don't have to be on your toes anymore."

Muttering, he reached into his pocket for his medication.

Carmen turned to Mac. "What was up with that detective?"

"I know he was hard on you, but believe it or not, Rutherford's a decent cop with a good record. He was just following orders."

"But what were they looking for?"

"Whatever they could find. See, the powers that be have decided that you're probably right—the threat isn't coming from Tio himself."

"Told you."

"Not Tio himself," JR said from the backseat. "But still something to do with Tio, right?"

Mac nodded. "There's a new theory—the drug payback one."

"The what?" Carmen asked.

"Your ex, before he skipped town, owed a bunch of money to some of the higher-ups on the drug chain. Nasty customers, trust me. They can't find him, so the theory is that by ordering your execution, they let Schluter know they mean business."

"But that's insane," she protested. "It would only work if I meant something to him, which I don't. If I ever did."

"Maybe so, but it's all we have at the moment." He stopped for a red light. "Meanwhile, the captain has asked for protection for you. Someone will be on guard by tonight. Will you be staying at the counselor's place?"

"Definitely," JR said. "What about the rest of the day?"

"You haven't been tailed so far today. I've been checking. Now, I have no idea just how thorough your assassin is," he told Carmen. "If they're watching your place, or JR's, if they have access to credit card use info, if there's more than one of them." He shrugged, met JR's gaze in the mirror. "Know what I think? Don't go back to your place until later. The two of you should get lost. In fact, as a safety precaution, take your car to a rental place, leave it there, and rent another one, then take a long drive. By the time you get back to your place tonight, we'll have two cops in an unmarked car keeping watch."

Now, he directed his tired brown eyes at Carmen; his gaze was both world-weary and kind. "Stay alert. Don't take chances. I wish I could promise you that we'll keep you safe, but the bad guys win more often than we do, so it's up to you. Got it?"

She nodded. Oh, yes, she got it. She might live to be ninety.

On the other hand, her time on this planet might not last another day.

Chapter 6

After Mac dropped them off that morning, JR took a pain pill and slept most of the day while Carmen drove them in a rented Taurus to the desert and back. In the early evening they wound up on the patio of Ciudad, a trendy restaurant with great food, thanks to two terrific female chefs. It was JR's favorite restaurant and he'd been meaning to bring Carmen here for ages. This small, safe oasis was located right in the heart of downtown L.A., protected from the traffic noise on Figueroa by high stone walls and foliage.

His shoulder felt stiff but manageable so he decided to forego any more pain medication; instead he ordered them martinis and listened as a trio played quiet jazz in the corner. He gazed across the table at Carmen, who seemed fairly relaxed. The drive, the day away from tension, had done her some good, too.

"How are you, Carm?" he asked quietly.

"Right now? In heaven. I love this place."

"Wait 'til you taste the food."

He smiled at her and she smiled back. He was struck by the picture she made: Carmen lit by the soft shadows of twilight. Blond, shaggy hair framed her pretty face, her large brown eyes, her pretty nose, her soft mouth. It was one of those moments he wanted to capture forever.

The martinis arrived and he raised his glass. "To my driver. Thank you for getting us here safely and in one piece."

She picked up her glass. "To my passenger and his miraculous powers of healing."

He chuckled. "Good thing the bullet wasn't very deep, but yes, I am starting to feel like a human being again."

"You look like one. Your color has returned."

"All I needed was a long car ride and sleep." He took a sip of his drink, savored it, then set it down. It had been a good decision to forego pain meds in favor of cocktails. "It's funny, when I was a baby, apparently I was colicky and the only way my parents could get me to sleep was to throw me in my car seat and take a long drive. Worked every time. Still does, I guess."

"Speaking of your family, how are your parents? You rarely mention them."

"They're fine. They're on a cruise at the moment. With a bunch of my father's golfing buddies. First class all the way, of course. It's how Father and Mother do things," he said fondly. "Hot and cold, running servants to see to their every need."

She took another drink, then shook her head. "Father and Mother."

"What about them?"

"You've always called them that—'Father and Mother.' Not 'Mom and Dad.'"

"They're not the 'Mom and Dad' type," he said easily, enjoying the camaraderie, the ease of conversation between them. Just the way it used to be. It was as though by mutual agreement, they'd decided to suspend reality and not talk about the events of the past week.

"Remember," he said, "they had me when they were quite a bit older, and they came from that New England Brahmin class."

"Yeah. They're nice, though. They've always been very nice to me."

"That's because they like you. You're not what they're used to, but they like you. Maybe not that first time I brought you home. Remember?"

"How could I forget? That huge house in Brentwood? A real butler and maid, this tray of cookies and fresh lemonade—squeezed from actual lemons?" She sipped some more of her martini, licked her lips, then chuckled. "And you were actually called 'Master Ewing.'"

"Which made you crack up and tease me the rest of the day. 'Yes, Master, No, Master, What does Master want to do now? Does Master enjoy Monopoly, or would Master prefer table tennis?' That evening, I put my foot down with my parents and told them we had to become less formal with each other." He chuckled. "They had no idea what I was talking about."

"I teased you unmercifully." Her smile was mischievous.

"Yeah, you did." He smiled back. "I needed teasing, Carm. It got me out of myself. It got me to see that there was another, more…casual way to live. You taught me that."

"I also taught you how to set off stink bombs," she said proudly.

"A most valuable talent to possess."

"Well, it's mutual, you know. I mean, this teaching thing. You taught me how to listen to a Bach concerto, you know, all about counterpoint and stuff? And got me reading mysteries. And taught me how to drive a stick shift."

Again, they exchanged grins. And again, he was reminded of all the years of being friends and showing each other new worlds, the fact that they were so different and yet managed to get along so very well. And how very much he cherished her.

"We're good together, Carm," he said.

"That we are."

He raised his glass again. "To our friendship. Long may it reign."

"Oh, yes." Again, they clinked glasses and drank.

Carmen had never held her liquor well, which was why she didn't drink much, as a rule. But tonight she would make an exception. The music was mellow; cool autumn breezes were offset by outdoor heaters. The drinks warmed her system. Being here with JR was— well, he'd always had the most amazing ability to make her feel special; tonight was no different.

Being here with him made her forget.

Well, almost.

"What's up, Carm?"

JR had caught her staring into the middle distance during a lull in the conversation. So she sighed and told him, "I'm sorry you had to hear all that stuff about my former boyfriends."

He reached across the table with his right hand, took her hand in his and squeezed it. "Nothing I didn't know about already." He rubbed his fingertips over her knuckles. "I was there, remember? Especially when each one of them became history?"

"Yes, but, I never told you *everything*. I kept some stuff back. And then, today, I didn't. I couldn't. That detective kept digging and digging. And, I don't know, I just didn't need you to hear about all my exes and their loser lifestyles, all at one time. It's a shabby little list. And it made me feel kind of shabby, too."

"Carm—" he began.

She removed her hand from his and held it up, palm out, to stop what she was sure was going to be some words of reassurance. "It's not about you judging me, JR." She wrinkled her nose as she realized that wasn't quite true. "Well, maybe a little. But the truth is, *I* was the one who didn't want to hear all those details today. It made me face the fact that, well, you said it the other night. My instinct when it comes to men sucks, and it's not a pretty picture. Time and again, I keep choosing the wrong guy. Men who don't really care about who or what I am, inside. Who don't value me."

"Well, then, all of them were idiots," he said loyally.

"But why, JR? Why did I choose them?"

"We've talked about this before. That little self-esteem issue of yours."

"Little?" She gave a derisive snort.

"All your life, you've always compared yourself to your family."

"Isn't that what every kid does?"

"I'm an only child, so I really don't know. But it's counterproductive as hell. I mean, all of us are better or worse or the same as the guy next to us. But to live your life wondering what rung of the ladder you're on keeps you in perpetual dissatisfaction. You're special, Carmen. You're like…sunshine. So bright, so interesting. And so loved, by your family, your friends. By me. Isn't that enough?"

His praise brought a pleased flush to her skin. "Oh, JR. You're the best. And right now, as we're sitting here, yes, it's enough." She frowned. "But then I go job-hunting or try to do a crossword puzzle or make my checkbook balance and it's not enough."

"No one can do it all. We need to respect what we *do* have, make it work for us."

She looked down at the table and played with a fork, pushing it back and forth. "Funny, Mom said something similar when I was up there."

"Grace is a very wise woman."

Out of nowhere, she remembered something she'd thought about yesterday. "Hey! We're doing it again."

"Doing what again?"

"Talking about me. We always wind up talking about *me,* about *my* problems. Why don't we ever talk about you, JR?"

He seemed taken aback. "What about me?"

"I don't know. Don't you have any problems you want to talk over with me? I mean, maybe I can help you with them."

"I'm sure you could. I just…" He shrugged. "I don't know."

She emitted a loud sigh. "Is this one of those

male/female things, where the woman wants to talk about *feelings* and the guy would rather have a root canal? Are we like that, JR?" She shuddered. "Like everyone else? God, that's awful."

He laughed. "Maybe we are just like everyone else." He lifted his glass, clinked it to hers, then drained it. "To being a cliché."

"A cliché," Carmen agreed.

He set down his glass then held up his index finger. "But, wait a minute. I did talk to you. Back when I was deciding whether or not to leave the D.A.'s office, remember? And you told me that if I didn't love what I was doing I needed to get out of there and find my— what was the word? My joy."

"Yeah. I remember."

"And last year I asked you about Eloise."

"That's right. You wanted to know what was the kindest way to break up with her."

"See? I have talked about myself."

"Twice is not a lot, JR," Carmen pointed out.

"Hey, it's a start," he said with a rueful smile. "One more?" He pointed to her martini glass. When she nodded, he signaled the waiter.

Boy, she was really feeling the effects of that first drink, and it felt great. Setting an elbow on the table, she rested her chin on her upturned palm. "What about Eloise? Why did you end it with her?"

Even though the expression on his face said he really didn't want to talk about this subject, she pushed. "Eloise was terrific."

"That she was," he agreed. "And…I didn't love her."

Carmen nodded sadly. "No, you didn't."

"Did you love Tio?"

"No." She felt a frown forming between her eyebrows. "Actually, I didn't love any of them."

"Why do you think that is?"

The question gave her pause. "I have no idea."

The waiter set down two more martinis and removed the empty glasses.

"Don't you want to be in love?" JR's question was said in an offhand, lightly teasing way, but Carmen picked up on its underlying seriousness.

"I guess…maybe…I've been waiting."

It hung out there for a moment or two before he said quietly, "Yes. I've been waiting, too."

Their gazes met over the table. Throughout the years of their friendship, Carmen had found JR looking at her with kindness, impatience, affection. But the look he gave her now was deeper and *way* more intense than any she could remember. It burned her with its laser-beam concentration. All of a sudden she felt squirmy, felt her blood speed up in her veins, was aware of little prickles of excitement darting up and down her skin.

Even felt her nipples harden.

Oh, boy. That attraction that she'd been aware of for a few days. It was back, big-time. She broke eye contact and glanced away.

Night had fallen, and waiters came around to all the tables, lighting the small candles at the centers. There was something lovely, mysterious, even, about the hush that evening brought, Carmen noted with the part of her brain that wasn't trying to figure out what was up with her and JR. Shannon had said JR was in love with her. But was that true? Was it love? Or plain, old-fashioned lust?

She was so deeply introspective—not a familiar neighborhood for her until recently, and just possibly alcohol-fueled—that when JR reached for her hand, she flinched.

"Sorry," he said. "I didn't mean to make you jump."

"I was just…thinking, that's all."

About me? JR wondered. About the two of us?

Just a moment ago, he'd seen her face flush prettily, even seen the tips of her breasts sharpen into small, rounded peaks. All of which had an effect on him, for sure. And all of which made him—despite the sore shoulder—want to thrust his fist in the air and howl, "Yes!"

He'd wondered the other day, when she'd kissed him. But now he knew. The sexual attraction he felt toward Carmen was not one-sided. She wanted him. How and when it had begun for her, he didn't know and didn't care, because it had always been one-way, and now it wasn't anymore.

This, he knew, called for a move on his part. It would not be smart to blurt it out, not be prudent to say, "Carmen, I'm in love with you, I always have been, and let's go to bed." No, he needed to do this more smoothly.

Carmen took a healthy swig of her drink. "Wow, these are strong." She was slurring her words. "Maybe we need to order some actual food. Whaddya think?"

He nodded to a waiter, who took their orders for four appetizer dishes and refilled their water glasses. JR couldn't help noticing that Carmen seemed to be having trouble focusing. He found that adorable. And sexy. He shifted in his seat as his jeans became too tight.

He held his liquor much better than Carmen, but this second drink was having a decidedly pleasant effect on him now, too. He felt an overpowering rush of tenderness toward this woman who sat across the table from him. Not to mention good, old-fashioned desire. An idea began to form in his brain.

She smiled at him with loopy affection. "I'm so lucky to have you." The slurring was more pronounced. "I've always had this knight in shining armor to look after me."

He emitted a small, ironic laugh. "Right. I wish."

And like that, the bubble burst; the reality of their situation hit him. Hard.

He rubbed his eyes with his right hand, then shook his head. "I am no knight, Carm, trust me. Especially now." He indicated his bandaged shoulder, which, despite the numbing effects of alcohol, was throbbing again. "And I can't help thinking about what we've been avoiding. You're still in danger."

Her face fell; she looked like a child whose favorite toy had been taken away. He was sorry he'd brought it up at all. But now that he had…

"You need more than a one-armed friend and two cops in a car to take care of you. Will you let me hire some professional bodyguards?"

"Are you crazy?"

"No. I am not crazy." He burped. "I may, on the other hand, be just a little drunk."

As though joining a chorus, she hiccuped. Hand over her mouth, eyes wide, she said, "More than mildly, here. What shall we do about that?"

It was a perfect opening, so he took it. "I have a suggestion, okay?"

"Okay."

"I can't drive because of my arm and I'm assuming that you're in no shape to get behind the wheel. Yes?"

She nodded. "Good, mature thinking."

"Which means neither of us should drive."

"The responsible choice," she agreed. "So do we call a taxi to take us to Santa Monica?"

"And leave the rental car here, downtown? Not to mention my actual car still sitting at the rental place in Culver City?" He frowned. "What a lot of cars."

"Three, actually. If you include the taxi."

"Didn't Mac tell us to keep on the move?"

"He did. But how can we? We can't drive."

"So, as I said, I have a suggestion. Why don't we stay here?"

"At the restaurant?"

"No. At a hotel. The New Kyoto is just up the street." Her eyes widened. "That huge, gorgeous Japanese hotel?"

"The very one. My firm does some work for them—if they're not full, I'll get us a suite. And I think you could use a massage. Me, too. Maybe." He considered the wisdom of that. "Unless it makes my shoulder hurt."

"I'm not sure."

"Why not, Carmen? It's Saturday night, we're on the lam from a killer, you've been tense all week, your life is in danger, my shoulder hurts, my muscles are sore, we can't drive. Let's just do it, okay? My treat." He put his hand up before she could get a word of protest out. "I can afford it and I'm insisting. Please, let me do this. I need to."

"But—"

"Call it an early birthday present."

One eyebrow shot up. "Three months early."

"Okay, then, how's this?" The trump card. "I saved

your life yesterday. So you can't say no to anything I suggest."

She didn't have a quick response to that one. Not at first. She gave him a long, hard look, then shook her head in wonder. "Wow, you sure know how to play dirty."

"Hey, I'm a lawyer. I know all the tricks of the trade. So? All right?"

After a moment, she managed a low-wattage smile. "All right," she said, then sighed loudly. "Actually, a massage sounds wonderful. But this late at night?"

"The thing about a first-class hotel is that they have twenty-four-hour service," he said with an expansive wave of his right hand. "Anything you need."

"It sounds decadent."

"Sometimes decadence is just what the doctor ordered."

"Ooh. Oooooooh. Oh!"

JR closed his eyes and groaned. For the past half hour, he'd been in the living room of a lavish suite, seated in an armchair, being forced to listen to the sounds emanating from the bedroom. Carmen, apparently, did not get a full-body massage quietly. Instead, she responded to the kneading of each new muscle group with vocal reactions that resembled the soundtrack of an X-rated film. There were moans and groans, loud, guttural sighs, the occasional "Yes!" and the always reliable crescendo on the word "Oh!"

He'd had a massage himself, but a limited one—feet and legs only—as his shoulder injury was just too new for any work on his upper body. He'd gotten thoroughly relaxed under the ministrations of an expert reflexologist. But his massage had only lasted a half hour; since then he'd had to endure listening to Carmen, the result of which was that he was all tense again, beside himself with wanting her.

He was dressed in one of the hotel's blue-and-white patterned kimonos. Unlike thick, cotton Western robes, the kimono was made of silk and was cut narrowly, not designed for a person to get lost in. So he sat in his chair, listened to the woman he lusted after with every fiber of his being and stared numbly at the jutting evidence of his lust, barely covered by the fabric.

He shook his head. This brilliant idea of his, to check into a hotel and get a massage, just might not have been the smartest idea he'd ever had.

Unless, of course, it led to one of his fantasies coming true.

"Oh! Yes! There! Yes!"

He closed his eyes and groaned aloud. Agony. Sheer agony.

Carmen felt absolutely delicious. Still tipsy and now glowing from an excellent massage. What a great idea JR had had! And how lucky she was that he was so generous to her. On her own, she could never have afforded one whole hour of deep-tissue work. The masseuse was a small, thin Japanese woman who spoke no English. It was like she'd known what Carmen had been through all week, and which muscles had been affected, and just what to do to ease the tension, the worries, the fears, all the tightness.

Well, of course, that was her job, to know how to do all that.

But still, she was truly gifted.

Carmen's body felt all smooth and slick from the oils used during the past hour. She wrapped herself in the pretty, soft silk robe the hotel provided, then smiled as she watched the small woman fold up her massage table, give a quick bow—which Carmen returned—and exit the suite through the door that led out to the hall. Sighing happily, she raised her arms over her head and gave a leisurely stretch, wondering how JR was doing out there in the living room.

JR. She smiled, licked her lips. She'd had quite a few titillating thoughts about him during her massage. Quite a few.

"JR?" she called out, opening the door between the two rooms with another contented smile. "You all done in here?"

The room was dimly lit. One desk lamp was turned on, casting all kinds of shadows over the walls and the rest of the furniture—a couple of love seats and armchairs, a long table, a state-of-the-art plasma TV. She raked her fingers through her hair—she'd even had her head massaged!—making it all messy, but who cared? The alcohol had turned off her brain, the massage had turned off her tension. Life just didn't get any better than this.

Sighing with contentment, her gaze roamed the room until it came to rest on the sight of JR, in shadows over in the far corner, sitting in an armchair, his bare feet resting on an ottoman. He, too, was wearing one of the hotel's robes. From what she could tell, the fabric had slipped away from his legs, which were bare. His nice, muscular, long legs.

Smiling, stretching some more, she ambled slowly over to the other end of the living room—it was huge!—

so she could see JR better. "Wow," she said, feeling like purring. "I can't tell you how wonderful that massage was. I had no idea how tight my shoulders w—"

She didn't finish the sentence—couldn't, actually. Because now she was close enough to JR to see, not only that his robe was open enough to reveal his bare legs, but that the part of JR's anatomy that was still covered, from the waist to the top of his upper thighs, wasn't exactly lying flat. Oh, no, not at all. There was a pretty major bulge there. Her eyes widened. Yes, quite major.

If her shoulders and neck and calf muscles were still humming from their massage, other parts of her body began to respond. She stared at JR's lap, unconsciously running her tongue over her mouth. "Oh," she said softly.

"Carm?"

With regret, she tore her eyes away from the silk-covered erection and met his gaze. He wasn't wearing his glasses, so she got the full effect of startling blue eyes staring at her smilelessly from under half-lowered lids. The look he gave her was hot and filled with a wordless invitation.

"Yes?" she said. Her mouth was suddenly dry; she ran her tongue along her lips again, but this time she did it slowly, deliberately, watching him. She noted how his nostrils flared, saw how his hands gripped the sides of the chair.

"How was the massage?" JR said, his voice raspy.

"Wonderful," she replied, getting all caught up in his gaze again and the challenges there. Her heartbeat quickened, her nipples were hard; interior muscles between her legs clenched and unclenched, preparing her, getting her ready. And they hadn't even kissed yet!

"How was yours?" she asked.

"I don't remember. All I thought about was you." His gaze roamed up and down her body, slowly, tantalizingly. "I thought about how you'd look without your robe, without any covering at all."

Quickly her gaze moved back down to the tantalizing evidence of JR's strong craving for her. "Wonder no more," she murmured, untying her robe slowly and letting it hang open.

She heard his quick intake of breath, which pleased her deeply, but kept her gaze on the lower part of his anatomy. "My, my, my," she said. "What have we here, JR?"

The room had been quiet; now it was filled with the sound of JR's labored breathing. Hers wasn't any too steady, either.

"See for yourself," he said.

Again, she locked gazes with him, and as she did, she slowly shrugged her shoulders and let the robe slip down over her body with a silken sigh until it was lying in a heap at her feet. She watched him watching her, followed the path of his gaze as he took her in, all of her, from head to toe, stopping at various points along the way to study her.

"Like what you see?" she whispered. Her nipples were so hard now, they ached; she felt moisture between her legs. She and JR hadn't even touched yet, and she was as aroused as she'd ever been.

"Very much," he said softly. "Carm?"

"What?"

He reached his right hand into the robe's pocket and brought out a foil-wrapped package, which he set down on his thigh. "Just in case," he said.

She nodded. "I think we can probably find some use for that."

Holy cow, she thought. It was the strangest thing. She and JR were going to make love now and she didn't even have a second of hesitation about it. It was right. It had been in the cards for a while. It was time.

In fact, she couldn't wait. She wanted to give him pleasure, as much pleasure as he could bear. Maybe it was the alcohol—all through the ages, the best excuse for unplanned lovemaking. Or maybe it was the heightened sense of danger she'd been living under these past few days. Whatever. If she had had any second thoughts they were gone. She was ready, she was more than willing and nothing was going to stop her.

Slowly, seductively, she walked over to him and sat on the edge of the ottoman. She scraped her fingernails lightly over his bare legs, then worked them up his thighs, just to the edge of the robe. JR closed his eyes and groaned; the bulge grew even higher. Carmen laughed softly. "It's like Christmas."

"What is?"

"There's this package waiting for me, and I don't mean the condom. And it's all mine to open up as I please."

He expelled a harsh breath. "I hope you open it soon, Carm. I'm on the edge here."

"Are you?" She worked her fingernails higher.

"I've been listening to you getting your massage. If I had the use of both of my arms, you'd be on your back right now and I'd be in you up to the hilt."

Her heartbeat was rocketing along now; she was wet and slick between her legs. "I guess we'll just have to improvise, won't we?" she murmured, then pulled away the fabric. Her own sharp intake of breath, as she stared, was purely involuntary. "Oh, JR. That's beautiful."

He wiped a hand across his mouth. "Beautiful?" he managed.

"Yes." She cupped a hand around his penis and gently moved it up and down. "It's beautiful the way it stands, so tall and proud." She used her nails on the sensitive skin, but gently. "Really, JR. All these years and I never knew this about you. I'm impressed."

His chuckle was strained. "I'm so glad you are. You'll be less impressed if this goes on much longer. I want to be in you, Carm."

"And I want you in me."

"Then what are you waiting for?"

He picked up the condom and handed it to her. She ripped it open, removed the condom and rolled it over him. Then she planted her knees on either side of his hips and sat down.

From the back of JR's throat came a hoarse cry of exhilaration.

"Yes!" she, too, cried out as he, indeed, filled her to the hilt. Interior muscles had to make room for him, but it felt so right, so perfect, having him inside her. She moved up and down on him, slowly at first to give him—and her—as much agonizing pleasure as she could, growing slicker and hotter with each movement.

She leaned in and kissed his mouth, took his tongue inside hers. He played with her breasts, reached behind her, squeezed her buttocks. And all the while she rode him, up and down, up and down, until the room no longer existed, until she no longer existed, but hung, suspended in some other universe.

"Oh, JR!"

"Yes! Let go, Carm. Please let go!"

And she did, flew up to the top of this alternate universe and exploded there. Moments later, so did JR. She felt him madly pumping into her, clenched her muscles around him to make it even better for him.

It was over way too soon, for both of them. She collapsed onto him, mindful of his shoulder, but unable to stay upright anymore. Her bones and muscles were jelly. Even as the sounds of their loud panting filled the room, she fell deeply asleep.

JR awoke sometime before dawn. He was in a king-size bed, lying on his back. For a moment he felt disoriented. He looked to his right—Carmen was sprawled out beside him. And that's when it hit him. Carmen was here, in his bed! It was hard to believe, but the truth was staring him in the face. What he'd dreamed of, wanted, craved, for so many years, had come to pass. He closed his eyes and gave thanks to whatever entity or twist of fate had caused it to happen.

He leaned over and kissed her ear. The swatting movement she made in her sleep made him smile. Next he licked her neck. This time she didn't swat him, but made a little wiggling movement with her hips. His smile grew.

Last night, as unbelievably erotic as it had been, had not gone the way he would have planned their first time together. His damned shoulder had limited his movement too much. Still, this was a new day....

This time he would make love to her, drive her as insane with longing as she'd driven him. He began at her neck and worked his way down her entire body, licking and kissing and tasting every part of her. By the time he reached her abdomen, she was making little noises of pleasure and urging him lower. When he moved his mouth and tongue over her upper thigh, she spread her legs for him and he dove in, eager to taste her. She was wet and ready.

He pleasured her, as she had pleasured him last night. Made her squirm as she had made him squirm last night. Brought her to climax with his tongue once, twice. And maybe he couldn't support himself on both arms, but after getting another condom, he lay on his right side so she could sling a leg over his hip and grant him access. He plunged into her; her cry of pleasure pleased him to no end. He worked her, teased her, slowed down when she was close, then sped up again. She was tight around him and it took all his skill to stay focused on driving Carmen wild.

Finally, he knew it was time. He quickened his pace; her hips matched his rhythm. He kissed her soundly, thoroughly, his tongue imitating the movement of their hips. Carmen emitted desperate little gasps, gripped him tightly, her nails dug into his back.

She erupted with a loud cry of ecstasy.

He felt a surge of primal male satisfaction before joining her, shouting triumphantly as he did, "Oh, Carmen! I love you!"

Chapter 7

Thoroughly sated, he was flat on his back, trying to catch his breath, holding Carmen close to him with his good arm. Her soft cheek rested on his chest; the hair on the top of her head tickled his chin. The position was familiar and yet not. It was all so new, so rich, he was moved as he had never been moved after lovemaking before.

He'd waited for her for years, and it had been worth it. Last night, he hadn't pushed; she'd come to him, willingly. The thing he'd wanted all this time, it was—finally—his. A warm peace filled him. They lay side by side yet connected, not speaking, for quite a long time.

JR was the one to break the silence. "I can't believe this has happened."

"Yeah, it's kind of weird, huh?"

He smiled. It was such a Carmen response. "I don't think 'weird' is what I had in mind."

"No?"

He squeezed her arm, leaned over and kissed her forehead, then lay back. "No. This was...special, Carm. It was the beginning of something."

As Carmen lay against JR's warm, strong body, she heard him but didn't really listen. The thing was, her head was pounding. Her eyes hurt. She felt as though she could drink about a gallon of water. She'd never been a graceful drinker—or rather, a graceful morning-after person—which was why she rarely imbibed. But she had last night. Oh, yes, she most certainly had. And her head was paying for it today.

From the neck down, however, she felt amazingly relaxed and deeply contented. Making love with JR, well, it had been like nothing she'd ever experienced before. Ever.

But as the words JR spoke registered, she got the meaning behind them. Right at the end of their last bout of lovemaking, he'd said, "I love you." And not the way one friend said it to another friend.

Just now, he'd said it was "the beginning." She knew JR really well, and what he meant was that, in his mind, they were now at the beginning of a *relationship,* and all that went with it.

JR was staking his claim. On her.

And he was moving way too fast.

Still, she voiced the question, just to make sure. "Um...what exactly do you mean?"

"Do you honestly not know?"

Yes, she did know, but, boy, she didn't want to hear it. Really, if she could have crawled under the bed and hidden there, she would have. Instead, she pulled her head out from under his embrace and lay on her back, separate and apart.

"Don't, Carm."

"Don't what?"

"Don't pull away."

"I'm trying not to. But, look, we've always said we need to be honest with each other, right?"

"Right."

"Then, well, if you don't mind my saying, aren't you kind of rushing things? This was one night. A night of great sex, mind-boggling sex. The best ever. Truly. Can't we just, I don't know, let that be enough for now? See what happens down the line?"

"It meant nothing else? Great sex and that's it?"

Even though he was trying to mask it, she heard the hurt in his voice, and she felt instant guilt. "No, I don't mean that. Of course it was more. Or, I mean, I think it was." She flung an arm over her aching eyes and wished the world would disappear.

"I'm not quite sure what happened," she said. "We had too much to drink, that much I know. But that's not really it. There's been this sense, ever since Peg Davis's murder, that I need to live my life, well, as though each day is my last. Sorry, I know that sounds melodramatic, but it's true. So what I'm saying is…last night was *wonderful,* yes, and *special,* yes. But I'm just not sure how *real* it was."

She felt the bed shift as he propped himself on his good elbow. She moved her arm from over her eyes to above her head and forced herself to look up at him.

In the dim morning light glowing behind the curtained picture windows, she could see him gazing at her, a thoughtful expression on his face. She knew just what that look meant—his agile mind was running through various sentence constructions, trying to decide how to phrase something. "Just say it, JR. Whatever it is."

Finally, he spoke. "Do you know how long I've dreamed of having you in my bed?"

Oh, God, she thought, panic rising in her chest. She really, truly, deeply did *not* want to know. But it looked like he was going to tell her anyway.

"From the time I knew about what men and women could do to each other, could mean to each other, it's always been you."

No, she groaned silently. *Don't put that on me. It's too much responsibility. I'll break your heart.*

"Do you know how many years it's been?" he went on. "How many times I've had to keep my mouth shut?"

The intensity of his feelings was overwhelming. They filled the room, like a tidal wave that would not be stopped. She felt smothered. "Don't, JR. Please don't tell me all this."

"You asked for the truth."

"Yes, but it's too much."

"Why?"

"Because it changes everything."

"Why?"

"We won't be friends anymore."

"Why not?"

"Stop it, please. God, you're relentless!" She scrambled out of bed and reached for the hotel robe draped across the lounge chair next to the bed. Couldn't he see? She wasn't in his league. He would get tired of her. It would end badly.

It would ruin their friendship.

But he just wouldn't give up. "*Why* won't we be friends anymore?"

"Well, because we'd be lovers."

"And the two are mutually exclusive?"

She sat on the lounge, brushed her hair out of her eyes, tried to quell the sense of panic. "For me, yeah, they always have been."

Holding his left arm to his chest, JR moved over to the side of the bed and sat, staring at her. "You're scared, aren't you?"

"Terrified," she admitted.

He seemed to relax then, offering her one of his warm, supportive smiles. "I'm not like all the other guys," he said softly, "and that's what scares you. You won't be able to get rid of me so easily. This time will be different, Carm, I promise."

"How do you know?"

"I just do," he said, radiating truly irritating male confidence.

It worked. She was irritated. "You know, you're talking as though something's been settled."

"For me, it's been settled for a long time."

She stuck her chin out. "And I have no say here? I'm just catching up. Think about it from my perspective, JR. This is all pretty new for me—you need to give me some time, some space."

JR, genuinely perplexed, had no idea what to do next. Or he wanted to do way too many things at the same time. He wanted to hold her, shake her, make love to her. But Carmen was doing it again, trying to push away the truth. Couldn't she see it? It was staring her in the face.

They were meant for each other. Why the hell was she fighting it?

He tried for calm, tried to sound reasonable. He was the lawyer here; he had control of his emotions. "Just tell me, Carm. All these years, were you completely unaware of how I felt about you? How much I loved you?"

His use of the three little words made her wince, which, he had to admit, took some of the wind out of his sails. Self-doubt began to nibble at the edges of his ego. Was he wrong about how right they were for each other?

Carmen lowered her gaze and began to pick at a thread in the lounge chair's fabric. "Not really," she said in a small voice. "I mean, once in a while, something would, I don't know, flash in my brain, that the way you were acting, or a look in your eye, it was the way a man would look or act if he was in love. But I always ignored those little flashes. They made me, you know, squirmy."

"Why?"

She jerked her head up, glared at him. "I've already told you. Weren't you listening? Because you were my friend. You don't think that way about your friend."

He sighed. "So we're back to that again."

"Yes," she said defiantly, emphatically. "We're friends. You're my best friend." She clasped her hands under her chin in a position of supplication. "You mean so much to me, JR. I don't want to lose you."

"Why would you lose me?"

"Well, because that's what happens. If we get physical."

Despite the sinking feeling in the pit of his stomach, he allowed himself a wry smile. "We already got physical."

"You know what I mean." Now her hands were in her

lap, gripping each other. "Last night was wonderful. Truly. Mind-blowing. But we can't do it again."

"Excuse me?"

"If we go on the way we did last night, it'll get all hot and heavy and it'll keep being be wonderful…until it isn't anymore, and then it will be over, and I'll have lost a lover *and* my best friend."

"You're sure that will happen to us?"

"It always has. You say this time it will be different. But how do you know? Neither of us has a particularly good track record, remember?"

Deep inside, a voice was telling him to put the brakes on. To call a halt to this entire conversation. To let it go, relax, give her time, just as she had asked him to do. He'd gone for a home run when he should have gone for a single. He was blowing it, pushing her away instead of drawing her closer.

He knew it with every cell in his body.

Except…he couldn't put the brakes on. A dam had burst inside him, and there didn't seem to be any way to plug up the hole. "Do you truly not get why? Because this is different. This is about love. I love you and I'm in love with you."

"Why?" she cried. "How come you love me?"

That stopped him dead, but only briefly. There it was. Of course. All that insecurity of hers, in one loaded, heartfelt question. He wanted to cry, wanted to take her in his arms and tell her how special, how loveable she was. He'd been doing that their entire lives.

But he couldn't fill in her empty spaces; it didn't work that way. She had to get there on her own. His shoulders sagged, the left one throbbing with pain.

"Oh, Carm," he said on a long sigh. "I'm not going to go there. I love you. That's all. I just do. And, you may not like this, but I think you're in love with me."

She stared at him, her expression troubled. Then she lowered her gaze again and went back to picking at the thread. "Don't tell me how I feel," she said in an aggrieved little voice.

He wasn't getting through. The woman was impossible. She'd just turned what ought to be an occasion for celebration and joy into sheer misery.

Not that he was acting too mentally healthy himself, with all his years of needing her hanging out for the entire world to see.

"You're right," he admitted. "Okay. Sorry."

But Carmen was just getting started. "I mean, there you go again, taking charge. It's like something's been decided before I even had a chance to think about it."

She was warped, yes. Feeling miserable about a relationship with a man was her home territory, sure. But JR knew she was right about this one—he was telling her how she felt and making decisions for her. Again. As he'd done for years.

"Dammit," he said, more angry with himself now than at her. He lay back on the bed, expelled another breath and shook his head. "Damn," he muttered. "This is not the way it was supposed to be."

He closed his eyes and turned away from her, and was greeted by a searing pain across his shoulder. He'd forgotten about the damn shoulder. Idiot! He tried to grit his teeth against the pain, but a moan escaped.

Carmen was next to him in a flash. "Are you okay? What happened?"

"Nothing." It throbbed like a son of a bitch. He rolled onto his back.

"Your shoulder. Do you want a pain pill?"

"Go away, Carmen," he said through clenched teeth. "Just leave me alone."

She went into the bathroom. He closed his eyes, waiting for the ache to subside. After a couple of minutes, he heard the door to the bathroom open, then a rustling noise. Then she was by his side again. "Here."

He opened his eyes and looked at her. She was standing next to the bed. She was dressed in the only outfit she'd had with her since Friday morning—the long, dark skirt and layered tops. She had a pill in one hand and a glass of water in the other. "Take this."

"I don't need it."

"Take it, JR. Stop being such a cowboy."

He took it, drank the water then set the glass down on the table next to the bed. And watched as Carmen headed for the door to the room. "What are you doing?" he said.

"Getting out of here."

He struggled to sit up. "No, don't leave. It's dangerous."

"I'm just going to get some coffee. Lie back down, JR."

"We can call room service."

"I need to be alone. I won't leave the hotel. I'll be back soon. Rest, okay?"

And with that, she was out the door. He lay back down, thoroughly miserable, cursing himself for pushing her, cursing her for pushing him away, cursing his shoulder for hurting and cursing whatever gods were now laughing at him from above.

* * *

The sound of an electronic key card woke him up out of a drugged sleep. He opened his eyes to see a small brunette dressed in some kind of bright coral sweats walking into the room. When he retrieved his glasses from the nightstand and put them on, the brunette came into focus. It was Shannon.

"Oh, good," she said, "you're decent." She was carrying two large brown grocery bags and a small suitcase, all of which she set down on the table by the picture windows. "How are you feeling?"

JR realized he was naked under the covers, so he pulled them up even higher, then he shook his head, trying to clear it. "Like I took a pill that knocked me out. But—" he rotated his shoulder just a bit "—I think it's loosened up a little. What time is it?"

"Noon."

"It's always a pleasure to see you, Shannon, of course, but what exactly are you doing here?"

"Carmen called me, told me what happened on Friday. The little attempted murder, the shoulder wound of our mutual friend. After I finished yelling at her for not telling me sooner, I told her I needed to see you both, to make sure you're okay."

"What's in the bags?"

"Lox and bagels. Brunch."

"They have room service here." He was still groggy, but had he said something like that earlier to Carmen?

"Yeah, but Carmen made a special request for Canter's bagels and lox, and when my sister makes a special request, especially two days after someone takes a shot at her, I'm there." She grinned; it wasn't the same smile as Carmen's, but when the Coyle girls grinned, it was hard not to feel immediately happier.

He ran his tongue over his teeth. Brutal. "Where is she?"

"Browsing in the gift shop. She'll be right up."

She pulled open the drapes and stared out at the vista below them—the tall buildings of downtown L.A., their windows reflecting bright sunshine today; beyond were small, neat neighborhoods of one- and two-story homes, and farther on, mountains and blue sky as far as the eye could see.

"Nice," Shannon murmured, then turned her attention back to him. She cocked her head to one side. "With my acute powers of observation, I can't help noticing that there's only one bed in this room."

"Good call."

"And that you and my sister spent the night here. And that you're lying in said bed without, I believe, a stitch of clothing on." Cocking her head to the other side, she offered a sly smile. "Is there something I should know?"

He kept his face expressionless. "Gee, I don't know. Is there?"

The expression "saved by the bell" didn't quite cover the sudden ringing of a cell phone, coming from the spacious closet near the bathroom, but it was in the ballpark.

"That would be yours," Shannon said, walking over to the closet and retrieving the jangling instrument from his pants pocket, "as my sister has hers with her." She flipped it open. "JR's phone," she said. "Who is this, please?... No, I'm her sister. And you are?... Oh?...

Yes, he is." She walked over to JR and handed him the phone. "Someone named Mac."

He spoke into the mouthpiece. "Good morning."

"Where the hell are you, Counselor? I've had two guys outside your place all night and they said you two never showed up."

"I'm sorry, Mac. I should have called you. I forgot. We're at a hotel. Any news?"

"No, but I thought I might drop by, discuss a couple of things. So which hotel?"

"We're downtown, at the New Kyoto."

Mac whistled. "Nice. I'm over in Ladera Heights, which is about fifteen minutes away. You gonna be there for a while?"

"Sure. We have lox and bagels."

"At a Japanese hotel?"

"Don't ask." Smiling, JR hung up.

Shannon sat on the edge of the bed. "Who's Mac?"

"The detective working on the case."

"You and he sounded pretty friendly."

"He's okay. He's coming over."

"That's nice. Now back to the previous discussion. About where my sister spent the night."

This time he was saved by the sound of a door opening and Carmen walked in, carrying a couple of pale blue shopping bags. When she saw JR, she smiled. "Oh, good, you're up. Better?"

It was an okay smile, he noted, just a little on the tentative side. Which made sense, because he was feeling pretty tentative himself.

This morning, postlovemaking, she'd been insecure and difficult to pin down, sure. But he'd been an ass.

He'd leaped on her, practically proposed to her after one night together. The opposite of smooth. Clumsy. Awkward. Insensitive. JR knew Carmen so well, he should have predicted she'd be thrown by the change in their relationship, should have given her time to adjust.

Of course, it was entirely possible that it wasn't that she needed time to adjust, but that while she found sex with him satisfactory—*mind-blowing* was, he believed, one of the expressions she'd used—she didn't return his feelings. In fact—and this was really depressing, but it had to be faced—it was more than possible. The sex *had* been spectacular, but that might have been because they knew each other so well, were comfortable with each other as people, didn't have to worry about impressing each other or looking good—the way it was when relative strangers connected.

Idiot, he called himself. Jumping to conclusions, forecasting a romantic happy ending with no real evidence that one was in the cards. Didn't he owe his best friend better treatment than that?

"Hey, Carm, thanks for making me take that pill. I needed the rest."

Her smile was broader now, happier. "Yeah, you were pretty grumpy. But then you've always been a bad patient."

"I just hate being fussed over."

Shannon was watching them, studying them, looking for hints. But as though they'd gotten together and planned it, neither he nor Carmen acted like morning-after lovers. Reaching into one of the bags, Carmen presented him with a toothbrush and toothpaste, a throwaway razor and an extremely colorful Hawaiian shirt.

"What's this for?"

"Do I have to have an excuse to buy you a present?"

"No. But I don't wear those. They're a little loud for my taste."

"It's loose and will be easier to wear with your sling. Shannon and I will turn our backs while you head for the bathroom. Put on the shirt. By the time you come out, we'll have the food set out. Room service is bringing coffee. I'll help you with the buttons. Okay?"

"When did you get so pushy?" he grumbled.

"It's pretty recent." She laughed. "And it feels great."

By the time Mac arrived, for once not wearing a suit jacket, but dressed instead in a pair of old chinos, loafers and a faded Just Say No sweatshirt, brunch was spread across the table. After he and Shannon were introduced to each other, he sat down and helped himself to a healthy serving of thick cream cheese and lox, and generous slices of red onion and tomato piled on a garlic bagel.

After the first bite, he moaned with pleasure. "When I was first on the force, I worked the Fairfax area, and that was when I was introduced to lox and bagels. Fine, fine food."

"You're dressed like it's your day off," Carmen observed between bites of her own creation. "Why are you here?"

"Because this case is bugging me. You might say I've taken a personal interest in it."

Shannon raised an eyebrow. "Really?"

He nodded. "Maybe it's because I'm two months away from retirement and I should be working a desk job, but I'm too restless to sit still. Maybe it's because I'm tired of people being victimized by guns and crazy people."

"Wow," Shannon said. "A cop who actually cares."

Instead of rising to the bait, he said, mildly, "There are others, trust me. And I'm pissed off because we got diddly on this damn thing."

"Thanks, Mac," Carmen said, making a face. "It makes me feel all warm and toasty."

"Wish it could be different. But, here's the thing. We need more digging, but our resources—LAPD's, I mean—well, they're stretched kind of thin at the moment. I met this kid a few years ago, one of those computer-whiz types. The kid could hack into anything. I busted him for petty theft, stealing parts at a computer store. Kid was broke, hungry, no dad, mom working three jobs, never home. You know the drill."

Shannon nodded. "I'm afraid so."

"The kid—Ben, his name is—had built himself a first-rate computer from stuff he salvaged. Anyhow, I busted him and he served some time in juvie. Then again, after he was eighteen, he served six months, this time for illegal computer hacking. I read him the riot act and I've kind of kept an eye on him since. I'm pretty sure his life as a career criminal is over. He found out he can make a lot more money obeying the law and fingering other hackers.

"Now, he ought to be earning six figures with some huge firm—and he's had offers, trust me, even with his record. But the damn kid loves to surf and he can't stand heights, so working in one of those huge office buildings freaks him out, and he won't be separated from the ocean. Anyhow, long story short, he lives in Redondo Beach, surfs the waves morning and evening and does freelance investigative work on the computer in between."

"And you think we should talk to him?" JR asked.

"I already did. He's expecting your call." He handed them a slip of paper with an address and phone number written on it. "If there's anything in Carmen's background, associations, whatever, that might shed some light on this whole thing, the kid'll find it. And after he does, I want you to let me know what he found. I'll take it from there. Okay?"

"Got it, Mac," Carmen said. "And thanks."

"One more thing," Mac said, holding up his index finger. "This is all off the record. Are we clear on that, Counselor? Both counselors? If you want to hassle me with invasion of privacy issues, then this conversation never happened and I never gave you anyone's phone number. It's my ass, not to mention my pension, if anyone gets wind that I'm using a felon to hack into the system."

Shannon gave Mac a thumbs-up gesture. "It's our asses, too, you know, as members of the bar. And this is about my sister's life, so your secret is safe with us."

"And, again, thanks," JR added.

Shannon glanced at her watch. "Oops," she said, and rose. "Gotta get out of here. I'm meeting a friend in Griffith Park for a power walk. So, we're agreed, Carmen, we don't tell Mom about this latest development? Until we have something concrete to give her?"

"Agreed."

"Where are you going to be today?" She shifted her gaze from Carmen to JR. "Both of you?"

"My place?" JR said. "If the police protection is still there."

Mac nodded. "It is."

"Okay, Carm?"

She looked at him, indecision in her eyes. "Well, for today, yes."

"I stopped by your place and got you some stuff," Shannon said, jerking a thumb toward the suitcase in the corner. "I figured you wouldn't be safe at home, in the near future, at least."

Mac nodded approvingly. "Good thinking."

"Okay then," Shannon said, walking toward the door. "I'll call you later, Carmen. And when I do—" she shot both Carmen and JR pointed looks "—I want some answers to the questions I've been asking. We clear?"

Neither of them answered her, so she said, in a mock-German spy accent, "Ve haf vays of making you talk. Coming, Detective?"

As the door closed on them, Shannon was saying, "So, you're two months away from retirement, huh? Ever thought about what you're going to do with the rest of your life?"

JR smiled at Carmen. "It looks like your sister is lining up some more volunteers for the storefront."

Ben was actually Benjamin D'Annunzio, although Carmen couldn't see a trace of traditional Italian features in the man—more of a boy, really—who greeted them at the door. He was a classic Southern California surfing dude—tall, lean and tan. His hair was sun-streaked blond and worn long, tied at the nape with a piece of leather. He had light-green eyes and a smile that could have posed for a toothpaste ad. He wore cut-off jeans and a T-shirt that said Surfers Do It Standing Up, and had an overall air of both innocence and enthusiasm. It was hard to think of him as an ex-con.

"Hey, guys," he said when he opened the door. "Welcome to my lair."

Lair was right. Carmen was instantly reminded of one of the sets on *Buffy the Vampire Slayer,* the room where those three creepy nerds invented all kinds of weird gadgets and plotted Buffy's demise. There were two rooms, a small one for sleeping, and a much larger one that was, indeed, a cave. It was dark, lit only by one weak overhead fixture and the glow from Ben's various machines. A huge U-shaped desk-and-table combination held computers, monitors, shelves of CDs, books and odd pieces of electronic equipment. One high-backed office chair on wheels was used to navigate the whole thing without having to get up.

On the console next to his computer screen was a half-eaten sandwich and an open jar of peanut butter with a knife across the top.

Ben retrieved two canvas director's chairs from a dark corner, opened them up and told Carmen and JR to sit. And then he got right down to business, asking all kinds of questions, similar to the ones Rutherford had asked—was it only yesterday morning?—but without the threat or judgment behind them. To most everything Carmen said, Ben answered with either "Cool" or "Awesome."

He took notes on his computer, including Carmen's full name, birth date, social security number. Names of parents and siblings. Schools attended. Names of other boyfriends. Jobs held. Names of coworkers. Names of friends.

She even mentioned Gidget. "She's a homeless woman who lives in the alleyway near my house."

"Alcoholic, schizophrenic, post-traumatic stress, or just a lost soul?"

It was a perceptive question—those were the main categories of those who lived on the streets, for sure—and Carmen really didn't know the answer because all of her efforts to find out had met with blank stares and avoidance. "She has a real sweet tooth," she said thoughtfully, "so it's possible she used to be an alcoholic. She's able to hold conversations, to find food for herself and her dog, but has a huge fear of being inside."

"Cool. And how do you spell that name?"

"*G-I-D-G-E-T,*" Carmen told him, adding, "I guess. I don't know why she's called that. Maybe something to do with the movie, you know, the one from the late nineteen fifties, early sixties, with Sandra Dee?"

"Sandra who?"

"You've never heard of *Gidget?* You should rent it. It's all about surfing."

"Yeah? Awesome."

She turned to JR. "Is there anything I'm leaving out? About me?"

He'd been quiet the whole time, but she'd been comforted by his solid presence next to her. Now he shook his head. "I think you've covered pretty much everything. Ben? Any more questions?"

"Nope. I'm cool. I'll get right on it."

Carmen stood. "How much do you charge?"

Ben grinned. "Nah, this is for Mac. I owe him." Still seated, he made a waving gesture with his hand. "Go. I have all your phone numbers. I'll get back to you."

"Do you have any idea when?"

Another huge, white grin. "When I got something."

* * *

He had something two hours later. He showed up at JR's door, dressed in a wet suit, one arm around an eight-foot surfboard, holding it like he would a date. "I'm heading up to Malibu after this. Can I bring my board in? If I leave it in my car, it'll be gone before I get back."

JR let him prop it in the corner, then he and Carmen sat on the couch while Ben, refusing refreshments because he didn't want to miss the "humongous" waves, sat in an adjacent armchair and read from his notes.

"Okay, here we go. I ran down previous boyfriends. One, Douglas Ripley, is in jail, doing time for trying to rob a 7-Eleven, which didn't work out because a cop happened to be in that particular store, buying a lottery ticket." He shook his head. "Dude had some bad karma."

Carmen nodded. "Poor Doug. Stuff like that was always happening to him."

"Two others are married, one with a kid up north in Portland, the other here in the Valley, North Hollywood. Works at a gas station, goes off-roading on the weekends. No records, either of them." He looked up from his readout. "Your pal Tio," he said, directing it to Carmen, "is a piece of work. Seventeen addresses in the past four years, five outstanding warrants in four states, one for unpaid parking tickets, one for credit card theft, two for drug dealing—one here, one in Montana—and one for failure to pay child support."

"Child support? Tio has a child?" Carmen felt as though all the air had gone out of her. "How did I let that one get past me?"

Ben shrugged. "Hey, some of these guys are real good at the con. They lie as easy as breathing. It would take an expert to see through it."

His words comforted her just a little. "Thanks."

He offered that toothpaste grin again. "No prob." In the next instant, the smile was gone. "Now, there's one kind of hinky thing I did find, but I'm not sure how much you already know about your background."

"My background?"

"I mean, some people want to hear the truth, no matter what. But some people don't."

Uh-oh, Carmen thought. "The truth about what?"

JR reached for her hand and held it tight. "Tell us, Ben. Whatever it is, Carmen's strong."

She turned to stare at him. "I am?"

"You are."

Their eyes met, and in his she saw support and strength and years and years of being the best friend a person could have. Whatever had happened between them last night and this morning, he was still her rock.

Fortified, she turned back to Ben. "Okay, then. Let me have it. Is it about me? I mean, am I...sick or something?" She followed that question with a weak smile.

"No, you're cool. It's not about you. It's about who your folks are."

"Mom and Dad? What about them?"

He blew out a breath. "So you don't know."

"What don't I know?" She squeezed JR's hand. She had a bad feeling, and wanted to stop the clock.

"See, the thing is, you're adopted. Sort of. Kinda half-adopted."

"Excuse me?"

"Your dad is your dad, but, well, your mom isn't. Your mom, I mean."

None of this was making sense. "What are you talking about?"

"Biologically. You were born in Tempe, Arizona, to a woman named Phoebe Kurtz. Gerald Coyle is listed on the birth certificate as the father. Phoebe died in childbirth. Grace Coyle adopted you when you were three months old. So you're, like, not her child."

Chapter 8

"Oh, my God," Carmen whispered.

"Hey," Ben said, "I'm not saying this has anything to do with what's happening now, you know, with being shot at and all, but—" he shrugged "—I was asked to find out everything, and I did. I'm sorry."

"No, it's all right," JR said, looking worriedly at Carmen.

"You sure?" Ben's gaze shifted from one to the other.

"Yes," JR assured him. "Carmen's just shocked."

"See, apart from all that—" again, he shrugged apologetically "—it's all pretty straight ahead. Carmen has a pretty clean life, all in all." He handed him the print-out of all he'd gathered, rose and said, "Can I use your bathroom?"

"Sure."

JR kneeled in front of Carmen. "Hey, are you okay?"

All she could do was shake her head. "I can't believe it."

"I know, it kind of came out of left field."

"Kind of?" She looked utterly lost. "I mean, just the other day I told my mother that I spent my childhood feeling like I must have been adopted. And that it was hard for me because I was so different from the rest of the family. But I knew that didn't make sense because I look so much like my dad, you know, the way Shannon looks like Mom. So I figured it was just my imagination, and I knew that a lot of kids go through that stage of feeling, you know, separate from their families and wondering if they were adopted but that they grow out of it. And when I was talking to Mom, she seemed...*stressed* by what I was saying. I thought it was just, you know, worrying. The way moms do."

She took a breath and blew it out. "Sorry. I'm babbling."

"Babble away. It's okay."

"But now I see that I must have pushed a button, opened up a nightmare. Why didn't she tell me, JR? Why didn't she just sit me down and tell me the truth?"

At the sound of the bathroom door opening, JR rose.

Ben walked into the living room. "Hey, you guys, I feel bad." He looked over at Carmen, still seated, her hands clasped in her lap. "I mean, I didn't mean to bum you out."

She returned his gaze and shook her head. "No. It's okay. Actually, it answers a lot of questions I've always had."

"Yeah, but bummer. You know?"

JR nodded. "Yes. Definitely a bummer."

Ben walked over to where his board was propped,

hoisted it and held it close to his body. JR joined him at the door and opened it for him.

"Oh, one more thing," Ben said, preparing to leave. "I almost forgot. That Gidget chick? She was in the movie. Played one of the beach bunnies. Her real name is Esther Lincoln, but she's listed in Screen Actors Guild as Ella L. Louise. Had a breakdown when her kid died— he was five and he drowned. She's been in and out of mental hospitals ever since."

Despite her preoccupation with Ben's bombshell, Carmen felt the back of her eyes prickling. "Poor Gidget."

"So," Ben said, "anyway, I left the report. It's yours. Later."

JR clapped him on the shoulder. "Thanks so much."

The blond young man shrugged. "Like I said, anything for Mac."

And then he was gone.

JR closed the door, then turned and looked at Carmen. Her suffering, her confusion, her pain, it was all there on her face.

All day, she and JR had avoided picking up the "relationship" discussion that had ended so abruptly in the morning; once again, he knew, it would have to be put off. Carmen needed him to be there for her, as a friend, a confidante, a rock. All the rest, the entire topic of sex and love versus friendship and love, was, for the present, relegated to the back burner. If he were a man who believed in fate and predestination, he would have suspected that there was some kind of cosmic conspiracy afoot to prevent him and Carmen from ever getting together.

But he didn't believe in all that. It was timing, that's all. And now was not the time.

"What can I do for you, Carm?"

She rose and walked over to the window, stared out at the ocean for a few minutes before saying, "I need to talk to Mom."

"Yes." He joined her at the window, put his good arm around her and felt her rest her head on his shoulder, the way she had hundreds of times before. "This must be so hard for you."

"Right now, all I feel is numb. It's so weird. I guess I'm…I mean, I *think* I'm angry. At Mom. Why didn't she tell me? Why didn't Dad tell me?"

"They must have had their reasons."

"Maybe so, but I need to know what they were."

He nodded. "I'm trying to imagine how I would feel if I just found this out. It's a lot to take in."

Her small laugh was utterly devoid of mirth. "You could say that."

She moved away from him, walked around the room for a moment or two before stopping at a painting JR had picked up in northern England once. It was an oil of a sailboat in the middle of the ocean. Wind whipped its sails and the waves around it were choppy.

She stared at the painting, hugging herself the way she did when she was feeling lost. The outfit she wore this evening, beige loose-legged pants and an off-white wraparound blouse, was unusually subdued, for Carmen. "Brave little boat," she said softly, "out there all by itself, but hanging on." She perused the painting for several moments more before saying, "I guess I should go to see her."

"Call Grace, see if she's home. We can be out of here in ten minutes."

She angled her head around to face him. In the fading daylight from his picture window, her face matched the oddly colorless quality of her clothing, except for the large brown eyes, now so sad that he felt a hitch in his heart. "You don't have to go with me, JR."

Don't be silly, of course I'm coming. You need me. He nearly said it; just a few days ago he wouldn't have hesitated. But things between them had changed. He'd heard her this morning—she didn't like it when he gave her "orders," didn't want him to tell her what she needed.

So instead he nodded his head once. "You're right, it's personal. Maybe it's best if I don't go with you. You can take my car. I mean, the rental car."

The disappointed look on her face said he hadn't given the right answer, so he segued smoothly into, "But if you want me there, I want to be there. And hell, what am I thinking? Of course I'm going. Have you forgotten? Have we both forgotten? You're not driving up there alone. You're in danger."

One hand flew to her mouth. "You know what? I had nearly forgotten. That other thing. That someone-is-out-to-kill-me thing." She rubbed furiously at her eyes with the heel of her hands, as though trying to scrub away reality. "Oh, boy. Remember before when you said I was strong? I'm not feeling real strong right about now."

"Of course you're not," he said grimly. "How many body blows can a person take in one week? We'll get through this, Carm. I promise." He walked over to a side table, picked up the portable phone and held it out to her. "Call Grace."

She took the phone and hugged it to her chest. "Do

you think this…parentage thing has anything to do with this…other thing?"

"I have no idea. Let's see what Grace has to say."

She nodded slowly, then straightened her shoulders. "Okay. I'll call Mom, make sure she's there. And then we can take off. What about our—" she jerked a thumb toward the window that faced the street "—protection?"

"Mac said wherever we went, they would follow. We're to ignore them, pretend they're not there."

"Well, I'm awfully glad they are. Two whole days with no potshots, no guns. It doesn't get much better than that, huh?"

He took her face in his hands and gave her a quick kiss on the mouth. "We'll get through this, Carm," he re-iterated, willing her to believe him. "You know we will."

"Boy, JR, I sure hope so."

The sun was gone for the day as Carmen and JR pulled into the short driveway that led to her mother's house. As soon as they did, a porch light went on, the front door opened and Grace came hurrying out of the house. Obviously, she'd been watching for them. The look on her face was tense.

"What is it, Carmen?" she asked, the moment her daughter threw open the driver's side door. She grabbed her by the upper arms and stared at her, studying her intently. "Are you okay?"

When the passenger side door slammed, Grace glanced over at JR. Her eyes widened in alarm. "JR. What happened to you? What's wrong with your arm? Whose car is this? Did you have an accident?"

She looked past them to where a plain sedan had just

pulled up to the curb. Two men sat in the front seat. "And who are they?"

Carmen couldn't help observing that this was not the usual unruffled, possessor of two master's degrees, salt-of-the-earth mother she'd grown up with. Mom was spooked, big-time.

But all of Grace's scattered questions about accidents and JR's arm had the effect of bringing home something Carmen had managed to forget: Mom didn't know about Friday's shooting. She and Shannon had mutually decided to protect her from more bad news, but the way Mom was looking back and forth, from JR to her, made her conclude no one could be spared the truth. Not today.

"I'm fine, Mom," she said. "So is JR. Those men are policemen. They're here to protect me."

"Protect you?"

JR took over. "Why don't we go into the house, Grace?"

The older woman's hand flew to her throat and she looked at one, then the other. "You're scaring me."

"It's okay, Mom," Carmen said as soothingly as she could, taking her mother's arm and walking with her toward the old house. Seeing the fear on Grace's face churned up all kinds of emotions inside her. This woman might not have been her biological mother, but she was the only mother she'd ever known, the only mother she'd ever loved. Still loved.

They seated themselves at the scarred rectangular table in the breakfast nook, surrounded by all kinds of family pictures that adorned the walls. Professional and amateur photos of Grace and Gerald on their wedding day, of all three adorable and adored Coyle kids at various stages, from infancy all the way through to the most recent Christmas, nearly a year ago.

Grace had put on a pot of coffee; they sat now with full, steaming cups of the dark brew in front of them. "Those two men outside," she said. "Do you think they'd like some coffee?"

"We're to pretend they're not there," Carmen said.

"Oh," Grace said. "I see. Or rather, I don't." She picked up her cup. After she took a sip of the hot liquid, she set it down again. "Okay," she said firmly. "You were very mysterious on the phone so now, tell me."

She looked from one to the other, and as though by unspoken agreement, JR took the first part. It would be Carmen's job—Carmen's obligation, she knew—to deal with the other.

"Grace, the shooting the other day that Carmen witnessed?"

"Yes?" She looked at her daughter, picked up her hand and squeezed it.

"The police seem to think that the original target wasn't the woman who was murdered. I'm sorry to have to tell you this, but they think it was Carmen. That's why she has police protection."

Grace Coyle's eyes widened, then her face drained of all color. "What?"

"Mom?" Carmen said anxiously. "Are you okay?"

She waved away her daughter's concern, then sat straighter in her chair. "Go on."

"On Friday morning," JR said, "someone did shoot at her. As it happens, they missed, but they got me in the shoulder. A surface wound, that's all. Carmen's fine. So am I. As you can see."

Grace's gray eyes filled with tears. Again, her hand flew to her mouth. "No."

"JR was a hero, Mom," Carmen told her. "He pushed me down, out of the way, which was when he got shot."

The older woman looked at her daughter, touched her face, her shoulder, as though assuring herself that she was still there. "You're sure you're okay?"

She managed a smile. "You're looking at me, aren't you?"

"And JR." Grace turned to him. "Thank you, from the bottom of my heart. I'm so glad you were there. But, how awful for you. I mean, your shoulder." She halted in midsentence; it was obvious that she was thoroughly confused. "But, why?" she whispered. "Why would someone, anyone, want Carmen—" she swallowed "—dead?" As she uttered the last word, a huge sob rose from deep inside her.

Carmen pushed back her chair and hurried to stand behind Grace, resting her cheek on her head. "It's okay, Mom," she soothed, rubbing the palms of her hands up and down over her mother's plump shoulders. "I'm all right."

While offering comfort and solace to Grace, she had the oddest flash of self-awareness. This must be one of those moments, she realized, one of those *passages* all the commentators and sociologists and shrinks talked about and wrote about. That shift that happened at some point after children became adults. The moment in time when the child becomes the parent. She'd read about it, but hadn't really experienced it yet.

Right now, all she knew was that her mother needed taking care of, and that despite her own personal trauma of the past few days, she was the one who could offer it.

It only lasted for a few moments—Grace didn't permit it to go on any longer. JR found a box of tissues in the kitchen and brought them over to the table. Grace wiped at her eyes, sniffled and tried to pull herself together. She gazed up at Carmen with a watery smile and patted her arm. "I'm okay now. Sorry. I'm not used to losing it like that."

JR said, "I think you're forgiven."

Grace clutched one of Carmen's hands and squeezed it tight. "You'll stay here. Until they catch whomever did this. Do they have any witnesses? Any suspects?"

"Nothing so far," JR said. "A figure in black, not much more."

"A figure in black," Grace repeated musingly, her brows drawn into a frown. "That's pretty vague, isn't it? Does Shannon know?"

Carmen resumed her seat at the table and nodded. "Yes."

"Why didn't you tell me as soon as it happened? No," she said, waving off whatever Carmen was about to say. "I know. You were protecting me. I did the same thing with my mother." She made a mock face of disapproval. "I should be angry with you, but I guess I'll forgive you, just this once. Just remember, I'm not an old hag yet. I can take whatever life throws at me. Okay?" She looked from Carmen to JR and back to Carmen. She smiled again, stronger now. "End of lecture."

"Mom, there's more."

Her comment wiped the we-can-handle-this smile right off her mother's face. This time she put both hands around her coffee cup and squeezed. "Oh, no. What more could there be?"

She *hated* this. Now that she was here, facing Grace, Carmen wondered wildly if there was some way to put it off to another time. But there would never be a good time, would there? And, although what she'd learned about her background a couple of hours ago was unlikely to be connected to the danger she was in at present, no one could say that for sure. Besides, Carmen needed to know.

"Here's the thing, Mom," she began. "No one has any idea why someone is coming after me, but there has to be some connection to me—to who I am, who or what I know, right?"

"I suppose so."

"So we did a deep background computer check on me, on—" she paused "—*everything* about me."

Again, Grace's face drained of all color. This time, however, Carmen had the sense her mother knew what she was about to say before she actually said it.

She went on. "So that's when I found out you're...not my biological mother."

No one spoke for quite a while. On the far wall of the kitchen, an old grandfather clock ticked away, sounding way too loud in the silence. Carmen glanced over at JR, but he was watching Grace's face intently, waiting for her to respond.

Finally she did, saying dully, "Yes. I see."

Carmen waited. And waited some more. But Grace remained mute.

She shook her head in disbelief. "That's all? 'I see'?"

Grace seemed to have gone somewhere inside herself, muttering more to herself than to Carmen and JR. "We should have told you years ago."

"Why didn't you?"

The older woman's head shot up, as though she'd forgotten there was anyone else in the room. "Your father. It was his wish that you never know."

"Well, I do know, so tell me about it." It came out more harshly than Carmen had planned, but that initial anger she'd felt at being lied to for so many years was back. "What happened? Who was my mother? I don't understand any of this."

JR began to reach across the table, as though to pat her on the arm, telling her to dial it back, but she shook her head. "Don't, JR. I want answers." She turned back and stared hard at Grace. "I think I deserve some answers."

Grace nodded slowly. "Yes. Of course you do," she said with a sad smile. She inhaled a big breath then let it out. "Coffee is all well and good, but I need a glass of wine. Anyone care to join me?"

Minutes later, they sat in front of the brick fireplace in the living room, surrounded by more family photographs, and some of Carmen's younger brother, Shane's, framed watercolors. JR had offered to leave the two women alone, but they both insisted he stay. They sipped their wine while Grace Coyle told the story.

"I have never loved any man but your father," she began, "and we had a wonderful marriage…or, at least, I thought we did. One night, nearly thirty years ago—" she smiled briefly at Carmen "—I came down to the den because I thought I heard someone sobbing. I figured your father had left the TV on. Instead, I found Gerald crying. It was when we lived in Wisconsin, before we moved to California. He was teaching at the university and I was going to school. Anyhow, your father was sobbing as though his heart would break. Watching him, I felt as though my own heart would break.

"I asked him to tell me what was wrong, but he just shook his head and said he couldn't. I was hurt. He always told me everything, or so I thought. We were friends as well as spouses, and I certainly had never kept anything from him."

She took a sip of her wine and stared off into space as she went on.

"So I sat down and waited. I didn't push, I didn't pry. I just waited. And eventually, he calmed down and told me. He'd had an affair." Grace swallowed once before saying, "No, that wasn't the right word. A one-night stand. The single time he'd been unfaithful to me, he swore. He'd been away at a conference in Tempe, Arizona, and had had too much to drink. He'd been picked up by some young woman and had spent the night with her."

She looked down at her lap, shook her head as though the memory, muted though it might be by the passing of years, was still a painful one. Then she directed her gaze at Carmen and with a small, bitter smile, said, "Needless to say, I was hurt. Devastated. Not sure what I wanted to do about the situation. Not even sure how much to believe him. If he'd strayed once, I figured, maybe there was a pattern. All of a sudden, I realized I didn't know this man I had married. I was terrified. I said I needed some time alone but he told me that there was more to the story."

Grace splayed her hand over her chest, as though trying to contain whatever emotion was bursting to be set free. "My heart stopped, Carmen, you must believe me. What more could there be? He'd already broken my heart, destroyed my trust in him, rocked the foundations of my universe. But then he told me the rest of it, and of course, my universe was changed forever.

"There was a child, he told me. An infant. A little girl." She shook her head back and forth. "And even then, the story wasn't done. This young woman, this one-night stand, had died giving birth to the child. I know it sounds archaic, even back then, but she had some kind of rare blood disorder—you didn't inherit it, by the way, we've checked it out."

Carmen nodded and said, "Okay, thanks," because, of course, that thought had entered her mind the minute Grace had spoken of it. "Go on."

"This young woman, she was estranged from her family, didn't speak to them, wanted nothing to do with them. The hospital had contacted your father, told him she'd requested that if anything happened to her, he should look after the child, to take the child. The child— you—were at that moment in foster care back in Tempe, waiting for your father to come get you. He didn't know what to do. He had no idea what to do."

Carmen found her eyes filling with tears. She could picture it, the pain Grace must have been feeling, the anguish her father—the most honest, trustworthy man she'd ever known—must have gone through. As Grace told the story, her own part in it, a small, almost incidental part, became less important.

Grace took another sip of her wine then cradled the glass between her palms. "I have never seen your father so helpless. You remember him—" she transferred her gaze from Carmen to JR and back to Carmen again "—he was so competent, so reliable. The kind of man you could always turn to in emergencies. Kind of like you, JR. Always there. Loyal. And solid. And strong. And he didn't know what to do. Except that he had a responsibility to the child, that much he did know, and he wouldn't shirk it. But he was terrified of my reaction and for our future together. We had one child, Shannon, who was nearly two. He was afraid he was going to lose me, lose her, lose everything.

"I told him I was going to leave, that I needed a few days to think about this. I took Shannon and went home to visit my parents in Boston. I talked to my mother." Grace allowed herself a small, fond smile. "Remember her?"

Nana had died when she was about ten, but Carmen's memories of her were sharp and filled with affection. "Nana was great."

Grace nodded. "So wise. The most down-to-earth woman on the planet, filled with common sense. I hadn't planned on telling her about this, but she saw I was unhappy and it all just poured out of me. She listened. She didn't tell me what to do, just said that no one is perfect, that I needed to find out if I believed your father's story or if I thought he was a man who lied, and then make my decision based on that.

"I wasn't sure how I felt about the marriage itself, not right away. But I knew some decisions couldn't be put off. There was an innocent, motherless child involved, one who had not asked to be born. I called your father and told him to go get you and bring you home. I figured, whatever happened, you would be better off with us than in a crowded foster home. If the marriage broke up, he would raise you himself. We both agreed on that."

Grace gazed at Carmen and smiled mistily. "And then the minute I saw you, I don't know, I didn't hate you or resent you. You were so sweet. So plump and adorable and lovely. The truth is, I fell in love with you." She snapped her fingers. "Like that. I knew you would be part of the family. If the family survived, of course. We told people that you were the child of old friends who had died in a car accident.

"Your father and I had separate bedrooms for months while we went into counseling. And at the end of that time I knew I had married a man who had had one slip, and that to punish him for the rest of his life for that one slip was not a reasonable option. So I adopted you formally. As I said, I was absolutely crazy about you from the moment I saw you so it wasn't difficult." Her smile was filled with sweet affection. "You are, you know, the most loveable person, always have been."

Carmen felt embarrassed, as she always did when hearing too much praise. But she said nothing, because all she cared about was the matter at hand. "Go on, please."

"Your father and I had reconciled, but he was still ashamed. He wanted the whole thing hushed up. As it happened, he got a job offer to teach at UCLA, and I was able to transfer my credits there, and so we moved to Southern California, where we simply presented ourselves as a family with two children. Shannon was too young to remember much, especially the fact that her mother's tummy had stayed flat but there was a new baby in the house."

Grace locked gazes with Carmen, her expression serious and troubled. "Your father asked that you never know. He was afraid of your judgment, of your scorn,

I think. Of all the kids' anger and scorn. He came from a pretty puritanical background, remember, and tended to be quite hard on himself. We fought about it, but he was immovable on the subject. In any marriage, you have to know when there's no chance of compromise and this was one. And so I agreed. I've honored his wishes. And I see now that when he died I should have told you, but I didn't want to dishonor his memory—it had been so important to him."

She rubbed her forehead. "And so you found out yourself. And I'm sorry. No one knew but your father and I, my parents and one or two trusted friends back in Wisconsin. Not Shannon, not Shane, only us." She spread her hands wide. "And that's the whole story."

The last gesture seemed to sap all the strength she had left. Shoulders slumped, Grace gazed down at her lap, as though waiting for a verdict she wasn't sure she wanted to hear.

It was such a sad little story, JR thought. There were no villains, just human beings doing foolish things, but trying to make up for them later on. Still, there were some missing pieces, and he was curious to see where Carmen went next.

"Was Dad definitely my father?"

"Yes. We had tests done."

"My mother," Carmen said. "I mean, the woman who gave birth to me. What do you know about her?"

"Very little," Grace said. "Only her name."

"Phoebe Kurtz."

"Yes." She raised her head. "But we can find out more. They have all these services now that search out the parents of adopted children. I'll help as much as I can, pay for it if you like. I owe you that." In the look she gave her daughter, JR could see anguish and fear. She was wondering if she'd lost the love of that daughter.

Carmen angled her head to stare at the glowing logs in the fireplace. Both Grace and JR watched her as she seemed to go inside herself.

"I'm so sorry," Grace said, her eyes filling. "The other day when you were talking about how you always wondered if you were adopted, I wanted to tell you then. I almost did."

"Why didn't you?"

She raised and lowered a hand in a gesture of help-lessness. "Because you seemed so lost, so sad all that day. You'd just witnessed a violent death and it shook you. I didn't want to add one more thing for you to be sad about. Pure cowardice on my part. I can only say that all these years I've been acting contrary to a core belief of mine, which is to tell the truth at all times, no matter how painful. Not that I'm blaming your father," she added hastily. "He believed strongly that what he'd asked of me was the right thing.

"I didn't agree, and I didn't have to listen to him, could have argued more about his decision, I guess. I only know he acted responsibly toward you, at first, but everything after that was motivated by love, and his fear of losing that love."

Grace hesitated, then said, in that forthright way she had of speaking the truth no matter the consequences, "And as I sit here, I'm terrified that you'll think less of me. That you'll be angry. Which, of course, is your right," she said stiffly, as though preparing herself for the worst. "I have no idea what I would do were I in your shoes."

JR looked at Carmen, wondering what she would say or do next. Fire crackled in the fireplace; for a while it was the only sound in the room.

At last, Carmen emitted a huge, audible sigh. Then she rose, went over to her mother, got on her knees before her and rested her head on Grace's lap. The older woman reached out a tentative hand and stroked her hair.

"I'm not angry," Carmen said, after a while. "I was earlier, when I found out. But not now." She lifted her head and gazed at Grace. "I'm a little…unsettled. About Dad. About the fact that, basically, I've been lied to all my life. It'll take some getting used to. But I do understand. Everything was about being human, not about being cruel." She offered her mother a smile. "And you know what? I think I lucked out. I could have gotten a wicked stepmother—instead I got the best mom in the world."

Grace put her hands over her face and sobbed quietly.

"Mom?" Carmen said, but Grace shook her head, holding up one hand as though asking her to give her a moment. Carmen gazed at her mother with infinite sadness and affection, then laid her head down once again on the older woman's lap, and closed her eyes. As it had before, Grace's hand drifted down to stroke Carmen's hair.

The scene was so heart-wrenching, so intimate, JR felt the back of his throat constricting. He wondered if he ought to feel like an intruder, because he didn't. The Coyles had been his second family for so much of his life that their story felt, to some extent, like it was his, too.

Again, he pondered how one false move, one mistake, had reverberations and ramifications that lasted a lifetime, not only for Gerald Coyle, but for his entire family.

Still, he had to wonder.... Did what he'd just heard have anything to do with the threat to Carmen? Or did they need to go back and start over, look at a different thread in the tapestry of her life?

He sat and gazed at the beautiful picture Grace and Carmen made, a golden tableau of mother and child in the glow of firelight, and prayed that the danger to Carmen would soon be gone.

And wondered what further secrets needed to be uncovered before that happened.

Chapter 9

At the sound of her voice, JR darted a quick glance at Carmen. It was Sunday night; Grace had insisted they stay over and he'd made himself scarce today, giving mother and daughter time alone. Now, he was the one driving them back from Santa Barbara, figuring that even with limited use of one arm, he was in better shape than she was. She hadn't offered even token resistance and had been, for the past half hour, scrunched down in the passenger seat, eyes closed.

"Hey, Carm. You okay?"

"That would depend on your definition of okay."

He smiled, relieved, even if only slightly. Carmen had been uncharacteristically distant. In a kind of fugue state. Depressed, he imagined. Overwhelmed. And he couldn't blame her.

He turned the windshield wipers on low. A fine,

coastal mist that was not quite rain was making it difficult to see.

"Talk to me," he said.

She angled her head around to look at him. The night was dark, the only illumination coming from the occasional overhead lamps along the road. A quick glance at her face revealed pale skin, tired eyes, downcast mouth.

"What do you want to know?" she asked softly.

"All of it."

She turned her head back to face front. "I keep trying to find a place inside my head where there is something, anything, restful." She sighed. "And I can't seem to find it."

"Yeah."

"You know how sometimes you stand outside yourself and observe your behavior? It doesn't happen like that too often for me, but that's what's happening now. It's like I'm watching myself. I see all these scenes in my head, like I'm switching channels with the clicker, you know? Peg Davis bleeding on the floor. You passed out, partway in the water. Mom's face as she talks about Dad's…infidelity. And—" She stopped, bit her lower lip as though not sure she should go on.

"And what, Carm?"

"Bodies. Nude bodies. Your body. My body. The dim lights in the room, you sitting on a chair looking at me like you want to devour me."

He hadn't expected that one, and he felt his groin tighten as the memory of her body came to him. Rosy and luscious, all over. "Yeah," he said quietly.

"The thing is, JR, it's all too much. My life…there are enough plot twists for an entire year on one of those afternoon soap operas. But it's all happened in a week, not a year. It feels...unreal."

"Yeah," he said again.

"And see, I'm trying to understand *why* it's all happening. Remember when I took that reincarnation workshop?"

"How could I forget? You kept doing these channeling exercises no matter where we were—walking, at the movies, at dinner parties. You would sit down and assume some sort of yoga position and close your eyes and chant."

"Yeah, well, it was a phase. There've been so many, huh? Still, if I believed in that stuff—which you convinced me was probably not something I needed to pursue, and I agreed—I would have said I was being punished for several previous incarnations, all in one fell swoop."

"I was having similar thoughts a while ago. But I'm with you—it's not about past lives or fate or anything remotely resembling any of that stuff. And none of this is your fault, Carm."

"No, not literally, I know. But it all centers on me. I mean, Peg Davis was murdered because the killer thought she was me. You took a bullet because the killer was aiming at me. Mom and Dad's marriage practically fell apart because of me. I can't help feeling responsible."

"That's not logical. The killer is responsible for the first two acts, your father for the third."

"What I'm feeling isn't about logic, JR," she said softly.

It was an old discussion, one they'd had many times. He nodded. "I know."

He waited to see if she had any more to say. Especially about that one other item on her list of the week from hell. Their lovemaking. She'd been the one to bring it up, so he figured it was okay to talk about it.

"What about us, Carm?" He glanced over at her. "Do you feel responsible for what happened between us Saturday night?"

She met his gaze head-on before he had to return his attention to the road. "Partly, sure," she said. "We were both on edge, trying to keep one step ahead of a killer. We both had too much to drink and we shared a hotel suite and we had massages and who could have resisted making love under those conditions? Especially with someone you know really well and who, on top of all that, has a great body and is really well-endowed? That would be you I'm talking about, by the way."

That last part took him by surprise. He shot her a startled glance. She was smiling. "It's a no-brainer, JR. No one could have resisted you."

She was going for lightness, he saw that. Keeping it on the surface.

Not his first choice. But he needed Carmen operating on all cylinders, needed her to be able to give that conversation her entire attention. So he smiled back at her. "Thank you for the compliment. I want you to know that I'm a lot better at lovemaking when I have both shoulders."

"I might not survive JR with two shoulders." She grinned now, her usual light-up-the-room Carmen grin. "Hey, that could be your Native American name. JR Two Shoulders. Catchy, don't you think?"

"Catchy," he agreed, signaling so he could pass an extremely slow driver. He'd removed his sling; the muscles around the shoulder were tight but manageable.

"Thanks, JR."

"For what?" He changed lanes and sped up, noting that three cars behind them, so did the unmarked police car.

"Letting me spill all the stuff in my head. I needed to do that. Even though, *again,* all we're doing is talking about me. It's a pattern we have, JR."

"Carm, stop. As you said, this has been the week from hell for you. Next week, we can talk about me all you'd like, okay?"

"Promise?"

"Promise. Now, how about doing some brainstorming."

She sat up straight in her seat. "Sure. Great. What about?"

"Why someone is after you. The cops think it's about Tio, but you don't."

"Right. Do you think it has anything to do with that whole adoption thing?"

"Offhand, I can't see how. But we'll pursue that avenue tomorrow."

"Good."

"For now, here are the questions we need to ask. What do you know? What do you have? What do you represent, that someone needs to silence you? We can start with the other names that Ben came up with." He looked over at her. "You sure you're all right to talk about this?"

"Are you kidding? Anything to take my mind off my mind. Sure, let's talk about Ben's list."

"I was thinking of jealousy as a motive. The wives or girlfriends of some of your exes. Revenge. You took their man, that kind of thing."

"Really? Huh. I don't know. I guess it's possible."

"Have you hurt people, insulted them? Have you sued anyone? Filed a complaint, gotten anyone fired?

Does anything come to mind? Something small that you didn't realize was important to someone else at the time. You know, people with grudges, short fuses, schizophrenics—now, in the past, anyone like that in your life?"

JR was firing questions at her like she was on the witness stand, but it was kind of fun, Carmen decided. She glanced over at him and shrugged. "No to all of the above. I think. I mean, no lawsuits or anything like that. How would I know if someone had a grudge against me?"

"But nothing comes to mind."

"Sorry."

He nodded. "Okay, then, how about guys who got nasty when you turned them down?"

"I usually try to do it with a joke, you know, because the male ego is pretty fragile."

One side of his mouth quirked up. "It is, at that. But you've been hit on quite a bit, right?"

"My share. I mean, I'm a female, JR. Still young and attractive enough to get some offers."

"Aha! So you admit it."

"Admit what?"

"That you're attractive."

"Reasonably, yes."

"Then how come when I tell you how beautiful you are you always scoff at me?"

"Of course I scoff. I'm not beautiful. It's only because we're such good friends that you think that."

"No, it's because you're beautiful."

"Am not."

JR took a moment or two before chuckling. "Okay, how many times have we had this particular debate?"

"Five hundred eighty-two," she said with a laugh. "I kept count."

That got another nice chuckle out of him. She couldn't believe it. They were okay, the two of them. Even after she brought up the lovemaking—which hadn't been easy for her to do, but it was the five hundred pound elephant in the living room, had been since yesterday morning, whether they'd wanted to admit it or not. So she'd brought it up, they'd kidded about it, gotten past it.

Was it possible? Could they actually still be friends after crossing that line into getting physical? Oh, how she hoped so. Without JR's friendship, she would be lost.

The mist had turned into rain, and even with a full moon and headlights, the road wasn't well-illuminated. JR turned the wipers up and concentrated on his driving. Carmen switched on the radio and found some classical music—JR loved the stuff and had taught her to appreciate it. Strings, sad and soaring, filled the car.

"What about Gidget?"

His question, out of nowhere, made her jump. "Gidget?"

"Back to the list of suspects. The mental illness theory. Aging actress, possibly jealous of young, nubile beauty."

"There you go again with that jealousy and beauty stuff, JR."

"Okay, but you know what I mean. She's not a stable person, Carm."

She thought about it for a moment, then shook her head. "But, you know, she kind of is. At least for a homeless person. For sure it wasn't her, dressed all in black, who pulled the trigger, that much I know. And I can't picture her *paying* someone to do the job. I mean, she's homeless. She has no money. Plus, it was her dog that chased off the intruder."

"Hmm. True." He snapped his fingers. "Aha! Got it."

"What?"

"Tommy Spencer, back from childhood to get even with you for pushing him into the mud puddle."

She slapped a hand to her forehead. "Of course. Why didn't I think of that?"

"And then there's Doreen O'Hara and Sheila Parton."

"Who?"

"You don't remember? They were the princesses at your high school prom when you were voted queen. They hated your guts."

"How do you remember names from all those years ago?"

"Legal training," he said with a self-mocking grin. "I have a mind like a steel trap."

"Well, mine's a sieve." She made a face as she remembered that long-ago night. "Boy, I hated when they announced my name. I didn't want to run for prom queen, from what I do remember. I didn't want to get up there with that stupid crown."

"I think that's why they hated you. You just didn't care if you won or lost—for them, it was life and death."

"They made the rest of that year torture for me. You were off at Harvard by then. You flew in special just to take me to the prom. My hero."

"Because Kevin Sims got sick and couldn't go."

"Kevin! God, I haven't thought of him in years."

JR smiled. "It was fun being with the queen of the prom. At my high school, I was definitely not one of the cool kids."

She slanted him a look. "You're definitely cool now, trust me."

"You think?" JR said with a pleased smile.

"I know."

Wasn't JR the best! As he had all those years ago, he'd stepped in, taken her mind off her troubles, even made her laugh. God, she loved him!

She loved him, she thought, frowning. But what kind of love was it?

It didn't last. He'd been able to distract her for a while on the ride down, but the minute they entered his condo and shut the door behind them, JR saw that she wasn't okay. She was, at least, no longer despondent; now she was more manic.

"That massage Saturday night was terrific," she told him. "I could use another one right now."

"If you'd like, I could—"

She waved him away, headed for the kitchen. "Still got some tea? I feel like a cup."

"Make that two," JR said, following her.

She put water in the teakettle and placed it on the stove. "I've been thinking," she said, "about the whatever-you-call-it, the assassin. Mac is sure it's a pro. But he or she sure isn't acting like a pro."

"Go on."

She found cups and tea bags and spoons and honey, and all the while she kept on talking. "Well, first of all they get the wrong person. And then, the second time, they miss. Aren't paid killers supposed to be more accurate than that?"

"Or aren't you just about the luckiest target in the history of the world?"

"Possibly. But think about it." She held up her thumb. "Monday, hired killer shoots poor Peg Davis, thinks he got me. Feels terrific, earns his money or whatever." Her index finger joined the thumb. "Okay, then a couple of days later, he or she reads in the paper the name of the murdered woman and says, 'Boy did I screw up. Got the wrong person. I'd better try again.' Which he does, on Friday morning, but fails again." Now her middle finger joined the other two. "He's still looking for me, but he can't find me, either because I haven't been home or he sucks at his job."

JR propped a hip against a kitchen counter and considered. "Add the fact that he tried to break into your house on Tuesday night, before he knew he'd gotten the wrong person, and was chased off by a dog."

"Or maybe he did know he got the wrong person."

"How? They didn't release the information about Peg Davis's identity until Wednesday. Remember? You were at your mom's and I called you up. It didn't even hit the papers until Thursday."

"Oh, right." All tea preparations in place, Carmen leaned an elbow on one of the counters and drummed her fingers against the tile. "Then why did someone try to break into my house on Tuesday night?"

Her edginess was making him edgy. "Either they knew they'd gotten the wrong person," he said, watching her, wondering where she'd go next, "and wanted to finish the job, or they thought you were dead and were trying to find something. Something you would keep in your house. Which leads us back to Tio having hidden something incriminating at your place."

She splayed her hands. "But I searched, JR. Thoroughly."

"Then it's something you have that you don't know you have. I'll notify Mac tomorrow, give him permission to bring in a team to search your place. If that's okay."

"Fine. Whatever." Her mouth quirked up on one side. "Maybe they'll find my favorite lipstick. Ringo Red. I misplaced it a couple of weeks ago."

"I'll tell him to keep an eye out for it," JR said dryly.

The teakettle's shrill whistle made Carmen jump; then she made a fanning motion at her face. "Boy, that scared me."

"So I noticed."

JR turned off the gas and poured hot water into the cups while Carmen began to pace back and forth in the kitchen. She was about as wound up as he'd ever seen her. Which of the many problems on her plate was responsible for the present moment's attack of nerves? he wondered. The danger she was in? Grace's revelations? Or the relationship between the two of them—what she wanted from him, what was reasonable of him to ask of her?

Whatever it was, he wished he weren't so aware of her, of the sensual way she moved, even when on edge. Of the way her blouse fit so snugly over small, perfect breasts that he vividly remembered touching and licking, driving her mad.

"Maybe he wasn't searching," Carmen went on as she paced. "Maybe he really was trying to break in to finish the job. Maybe he had some way of knowing that he'd hit the wrong target." She stood still and snapped her fingers. "Maybe he hung around after the shooting and saw me, with Mac or with you. You know. At the mall. So he knew I was still alive and was trying to finish the job."

"Either way, he wasn't successful," he reminded her. "It didn't happen."

"We're both calling the shooter 'he.' But it could have been a 'her.'"

"Could have been."

She was back to pacing. And his body was reacting to her as though he were seventeen again, when he walked around much of the day in pain due to hormonal activity in the groin area. Most anything could have set it off back then—a girl's smile, the rear view of a woman in tight jeans, the smell of perfume, watching a female rake her fingers through her long hair.

He was far from that boy now; he had more control than this, he told himself, and he'd better make use of it and soon.

"So he or she screws up three times," Carmen was saying. "Gets the wrong person, is chased away by a dog, hits heroine's best friend instead of heroine…who, by the way, hasn't been home since, so if he's been trying to finish the job he has to be really frustrated. You know something, JR? If he wasn't out to end my life I might almost feel sorry for him…or her."

JR handed her a cup of hot tea. "Seriously?"

"No." She offered a small, not-quite-successful smile. "Just injecting a little levity into the situation. Boy, this whole thing sucks, big-time."

"That it does. Drink your tea, Carm."

She took a sip, then set it down on the counter and hugged herself. "The truth is, I'm all over the place tonight, JR. Sorry. I feel kind of disoriented. I'm...I'm scared. What a concept, huh? I'm trying not to be, but I am."

That was his cue. He was supposed to go over to her now and hug her, offer his shoulder to lean on, murmur soothing words in her ear. But he couldn't do it, couldn't seem to get control of his body, which, recently allowed access to Carmen's soft curves and mysterious places, didn't want to behave, not this time. It had experienced paradise and it wanted to go there again.

Now.

JR took his tea and headed out of the kitchen, saying, "I know, Carm, but you're safe here. No one can get to you here."

She followed. "Where are you going?"

"It's time for bed. You must be exhausted and I have to get up early in the morning."

He went into his bedroom, set the teacup on top of his dresser, pulled open a drawer, took out a T-shirt. Then he went over to his bed, grabbed one of the pillows and walked into the living room.

Carmen followed him again. "What are you doing?"

"Getting ready for bed." He walked over to the linen closet and grabbed a couple of blankets, went back to the living room and spread them on the couch.

She perched on the arm of an upholstered chair, watching him, cradling her teacup, a look of confusion on her face. "Are you angry at me, JR?"

He looked up from setting up his sleeping quarters. "What? No."

"You seem to be."

He stood up, wiped his mouth and considered what to do and/or say. He didn't feel very smart at the moment. He was tired, his shoulder was aching, he'd been trying to be supportive and loving to his friend, all the while wanting to jump her bones again.

He expelled a breath, then sat down on the couch and gazed at her. "I'm not angry at you, Carm. If anything, I'm angry at myself."

"Why?"

"Because, despite everything, all I want to do is make love to you again. And again. And again."

Her eyes widened. "Oh." Then a small smile played in the corner of her mouth. "I wouldn't mind. Who am I kidding? I'd love it."

She stood, set down her tea and reached for the ties of her wraparound blouse.

"Don't."

She looked up, startled. "What?"

"We're not going to make love."

Huge, confused eyes met his. "We aren't?"

He took another deep breath. He was feeling sad, so sad. Probably just exhaustion, but it felt different. It felt...hopeless. "No. Not until this crisis in your life is over and you and I can talk. About us. The two of us."

"I see." She lowered her arms to her sides. "No, I don't. Explain."

He tried to deflect her. "Can't this wait? We're both tired and scared. We both might say things we don't mean."

"But, I'm curious. Why can't we make love? We're here, we turn each other on." She smiled. "It's way better than a massage."

"Lovemaking as physical therapy."

"Oh, JR, that was a joke. You know it's more than that."

"Is it? To you?"

She stared at him as though trying to figure him out. Then she nodded her head. "You *are* angry at me, aren't you? Because when you said you loved me the other night, I didn't say it back."

He considered her statement and had to admit there was some truth in it. "Maybe partly," he said. "Yes. It hurt."

"I never want to hurt you, JR. Never. It's just that I need time," she told him, hands clasped under her chin. "Why can't you give me some time?" All of the nervous energy humming through her seemed to disappear at once. As though someone had let all the air out of a balloon, her entire body sagged, and he saw how deeply exhausted she was; she could barely lift her head to look at him.

"Carm, please, let's not—"

"I'm overwhelmed here, JR," she went on as though he hadn't spoken. "It's really too much to think about. Someone is trying to kill me. And I just found out my mother isn't my mother. And I can't go home because it's not safe. And even before all this happened, I was looking for a career. Some meaning in my life? I have debts. I sold my car. I'm tired of it all. I'm tired of me." Her eyes filled. "I just don't want to be *me* right now. That's why I thought it might be nice to make love with you. Or one of the reasons, I guess. I was looking for some relief, someplace to hide from being me. To feel safe. I feel safe with you. Or I used to, anyway."

Making love with him to hide, for relief, because she felt safe. It didn't get much further away from what JR wanted to hear than that. That same sense of hopelessness swept over him again. "We're not talking about the same thing. We're just not on the same page."

"See?" She shook her head. "Just what I said would happen, it's happening. The friendship is in trouble. Maybe it's over. I hope not, but it sure is having a rough patch. And it's all because we got physical."

"No." He wasn't at all angry anymore. "It's all because I said something I've been keeping back for years. It's because I told the truth. And I'm sorry, Carm. If a friendship can't survive one of the friends telling the other the truth, then it has no excuse to exist at all."

"But—"

It was his turn to interrupt her. He held up a hand. "Please, Carm. Neither of us can keep our eyes open. Go to sleep. My turn on the couch. We'll talk tomorrow, okay?" He rose and headed for the bathroom. "We'll get through this, I promise."

"You always say that," he heard her say behind him.

"And I always mean it."

Something woke her up. The rattling of hangers. She opened one eye to stare at the clock. Six a.m. The noise was JR rooting around in his closet.

"What are you looking for?" she asked groggily.

"Sorry. I didn't mean to wake you up. I was trying to find a tie. Go back to sleep."

She flicked on the lamp, rubbed her hand over her face. Then she propped up her pillow—causing Owl, curled up on one end of it, to protest—and gazed at JR through only partly opened eyes. He was showered and shaved, and natty as always in a navy-blue suit and a pale olive-colored shirt. She yawned. "It's so early."

"I have to get to the office, make sure I still have a job."

"Are you serious?"

"Not really. It's just, well, last week, I wasn't exactly available to my clients."

An instant spear of guilt hit her. "I'm sorry."

"Don't be. Emergencies are emergencies. Everyone has them. My bosses understand. I have some work to catch up on, that's all. Found it."

He pulled out a tie; it was a deep-olive color with small blue-and-white-diamond shapes scattered all over it. He slung it around his neck, letting it hang loose.

Remembering his sore shoulder, Carmen said, "Need some help with that?"

"No, Daisy will tie it for me when I get in. Go back to sleep."

She frowned, scratched her head. "I smell coffee."

"It's brewing. It'll be ready in a few minutes. I have to go." He walked over to her, leaned over and gave her a kiss on the cheek. "Stay here, okay? Don't go any-where. Watch movies, read, rest. I'll call you later."

He walked briskly out of the room. She wanted to call him back, wanted to talk about how they'd left it last night, wanted to make sure they were okay. He'd acted like they were okay, hadn't he? All domestic and bustling around looking for a tie, coffee brewing, giving the little woman a kiss before heading out to slay dragons.

Weird. Like an old Doris Day movie. She shook her head. Weird.

Chapter 10

Carmen pushed the pillow away. It smelled of JR. His scent, his aftershave. It was interfering with her sleep. God, all she wanted to do was sleep!

She opened one eye. Seven a.m. She'd drifted off after JR left, and she must have had a bad dream, because she was drenched in sweat, her heart racing.

She pushed off the covers, gathered the cat in her arms and headed for the living room. Her heart was pounding, her head was filled with nonsense, buzz, lint. She made for the big windows and JR's million-dollar view of the Pacific Ocean. The morning sky was overcast—was there more rain forecast for today?

Her heart was beating way too fast. Was she having a panic attack? It sure felt like it. Once, during one of her many searches for meaning in her life, she'd attended a meditation workshop, which hadn't worked

out because she'd had trouble sitting still long enough
to concentrate. But she did remember that they'd said
to find a focus point, stare at it, and regulate your
breathing. Deep breath in, deep breath out, several
times in a row.

So she tried it. Stroked the cat's head, stared at a lone
palm tree in the distance, and slowly breathed in, then out.
In, then out. And after a while, amazingly enough, she felt
herself calming down, sensed the jumble in her head dis-
integrating, smoothing out, becoming manageable.

Her thoughts cleared enough for her to remember
that she and JR had had an awkward sort of discussion,
sort of fight, about the relationship thing. As she pic-
tured that vulnerable look on JR's face when she'd made
a lame joke about lovemaking being better than a
massage, she wanted to cry. She'd hurt him.

What was it with JR and this whole fantasy he had
about the two of them? The one where she would
suddenly realize how deeply in love with him she was
and would fall into his arms, and, like that, start the
babies and the house in the suburbs? Cue the strings.

This was so weird, a real role reversal. Weren't men
the ones who didn't want to commit too soon, and
weren't women the ones who *wanted* that commitment?
JR, usually the logical and unsentimental one of the
two of them, was, in this instance, the total romantic.
And she, Carmen, whose emotions and hormones had
ruled most of her life, was just the opposite, not allowing
herself to be swept away, asking for time to consider.
The old shoe-on-the-other-foot thing. JR being emotional, Carmen being rational.

Or…maybe not rational. Maybe terrified. She'd

admitted as much, to JR, to herself. Just what she was terrified about, she really wasn't sure.

What did she want to do about this? Whenever she'd encountered romantic problems in the past, Carmen's pattern was to avoid controversy and confrontation by just running away. If he were any other guy, she would simply become unavailable. Not return phone calls. Just…not deal with it. But this was JR. She couldn't *not* deal with JR.

Who was in love with her.

Or who, at least, *said* he was in love with her. She wasn't sure she believed him—he might be mixing up desire with love. But that didn't matter, because *he* believed it.

Did she love him? Well, sure. But was she in love with him? How did that kind of love feel? Was she missing some key element in her makeup? He'd asked her why she'd never fallen in love and she'd said she'd been waiting. Was that the truth? Had she been waiting? For JR?

Her brain hurt. Really. She wasn't used to this kind of self-analysis. She wished she had answers. To everything. Why someone wanted her dead. What kind of person her biological mother was. Why JR loved her. And if she loved JR.

Lastly, what would she be when she grew up?

She rubbed her nose on Owl's soft head and walked over to the picture of the ship. It had, for some reason, always called to her. As she gazed at it, she realized why. The little ship was her. Carmen was, as JR had said, strong. Whatever chaos life threw at her, she always survived. Maybe not gracefully, but still, she'd gotten through.

She'd also gotten into the habit of leaning on JR and,

recently, Mac. Shannon, too. Turning to them to fix her, protect her, do her thinking for her, when she was perfectly capable of doing it herself.

With all that had happened this past week, others would have had a complete breakdown. Not Carmen. Sure, she'd done a little falling apart, but not for long periods. After each blow, she'd bounced back, ready to take on whatever was next. So she needed to stop whining and shaking and getting all lost inside her head. She needed to stop feeling so passive.

She needed to take action.

Heading for the kitchen and the hot coffee, she considered her options. Her would-be killer was invisible, so she couldn't exactly take any action against him or her. She and JR had discussed all kinds of theories last night, but they were all just that, theories—how did you take action against something that wasn't concrete?

There *was* one place she could take action though. She could find out more about her biological origins. On her own, of course. No JR. She'd been taking up way too much of his time for an entire week.

The Kurtz connection was the next step. And she would take it. Alone.

Right after she had coffee.

JR listened as his home phone rang and rang before the machine picked up. After he heard the outgoing message, he said, "Carmen? It's me. Pick up if you can hear this."

He waited, but the phone wasn't picked up. She could be in the shower, he told himself. Or still sleeping. She was fine, of course she was. But just to be safe, he called her cell phone. No answer there, either, so, keeping his tone casual, he left her a message on her voice mail to call him right away.

He sat at his desk, stared out the window and told himself there was no need to panic. She would call him back in a few minutes. All he had to do was wait.

After Carmen said goodbye to Ben, she stood in the doorway of his apartment building and looked up and down the street. No men in parked cars, no out-of-place pedestrians. She was still wearing the disguise she'd cobbled together from JR's closet this morning—old gray sweats, a black wig from when he'd gone as Moe to a Three Stooges New Year's Party, a pair of ugly, black-rimmed glasses. She looked nothing like herself, and so far, the disguise had done the trick of keeping her safe. Not even her police protection had recognized her as she'd left JR's Santa Monica condo and gotten into a taxi to come here.

Not that she was complaining, but what had happened to her would-be killer? Was he or she truly incompetent, or had someone changed his or her mind about the need for her violent death? Theory number two was the definite winner. Wouldn't it be great if this whole thing just…went away?

She glanced down at the information Ben had gotten for her this morning after her knocking on his door had woken him from a sound sleep. She would have called, of course, but JR had the number and she'd been determined not to bother him.

The Kurtz family lived in Scottsdale, Arizona. Her grandfather's name was Hiram Kurtz, age ninety-one, confined to a wheelchair. His wife, Phyllis Canter Kurtz, died five years ago. Phoebe had an older sister, Barbara, married name Gale, three kids. On the paper was Hiram's home address. Also the name of the family lawyer, Peter Hausner, also in Scottsdale.

Which meant, next stop, LAX.

Keeping an eye on the street from Ben's doorway, Carmen called for another taxi. She would head to the airport, making a quick stop at an ATM to withdraw a whole bunch of cash. Good thing she'd sold her car; there was plenty of money in her account.

For once.

JR tried to study his notes for his upcoming court appearance on behalf of Angel Lipsky, a laboratory technician and part-time inventor with a lawsuit against a huge drug company for infringement of copyright. It was a fairly straight matter—the drug company, in its arrogance, had left a paper trail a mile wide—but he was having a terrible time concentrating. Carmen hadn't called him back, and he didn't know what to make of that fact.

Was she at his place and avoiding him? Had she left his condo? If so, had it been of her own volition? Or had the police protection failed and was she now lying on the floor, dead?

He was aware his imagination had headed straight for the worst possible scenario, but he couldn't seem to help himself. Things between them were so unsettled; now that he wasn't in contact with her, it was even worse. He'd called again, twice, actually, but she wasn't answering her phone, and the damn message center was full again, so he couldn't leave word. He'd also called Mac and left a message for him. Should he call Shannon? Maybe she knew where her sister was.

Why, all those years ago when he'd first met the Coyle sisters, why hadn't he picked the bright, relatively stable, together, high-achieving one to fall in love with, instead of the quirky, intelligent but underachieving, disorganized and forgetful one?

The answer, of course, was that there never was an answer to that kind of question. It just was, that was all.

He finally picked up the phone to call Shannon, but in the serendipitous way that life sometimes works, he was interrupted by his secretary, telling him that Carmen was calling. He punched in line two, then the speakerphone, and barked, "Where are you?"

There was a moment before she answered and he wondered if she was considering hanging up on him. So he said quickly, "Sorry, Carm. I've been kind of worried."

"Then I'm sorry, too, JR. I meant to call earlier, but I've been so busy."

"I called your cell a couple of times."

"You have? Oh, that's right. I turned off the ringer last night. I'll turn it right back on, promise."

"You're okay?"

"Just fine. I'm at the airport."

"Excuse me?"

"I'm flying out to Phoenix." He could hear the grin in her voice as she went on. "That's where my birth mother's family is and I kind of want to nose around. I've been real careful, JR, promise. I didn't use a credit card, so they can't trace me. I'm sure no one's following me. I've got a great disguise!"

"Well, good," he said, not quite sharing her enthusiasm. "I wish you'd waited for me. I would have gone with you."

"But you had to go to work. And face it, JR, I've taken up way too much of your time lately. You can't always be taking care of me. I'm fine. Please believe me. I'm just fine."

He wanted to believe her, tried very hard to believe her. "Do me a favor, then. Clear your messages so I can leave word for you if I need to."

"Oh, did I do that again?"

"I'm afraid so."

"Will do. Hey," she said cheerfully, "I can't reform all at once, but I'm working on it. Be patient with me, JR. Okay? Bye now." And then she hung up.

Okay, he told himself. She wasn't dead. She'd been funny and sweet on the phone, so she wasn't angry with him. This was good. He could relax now, go back to his trial prep.

He glanced again at his notes, but he kept replaying the phone conversation in his head instead. She was off to Phoenix. In disguise. What kind of disguise? Where in Phoenix? Did she have a destination or was she just figuring on walking the streets and seeing if someone named Kurtz popped up?

No, that wasn't fair. Carmen had a plan, of course. She was going to "nose around." What the hell did that mean? And why hadn't she shared more details with him? Because she owed him nothing, that's why. He'd told her she needed to take some responsibility for herself and, wouldn't you know it, she'd listened to him.

And like that, he was back to worrying again.

* * *

Downtown Scottsdale was a hodgepodge of what looked like 1950s-style adobe gift shops and sleeker, more modern restaurants and galleries. Camelback Mountain rose in the distance. The offices of Chernoff, Morgan and Hausner were in a pretty, three-story, Spanish-style building on a side street right off the main drag. Before she went in, Carmen grabbed a cup of coffee and a donut in a nearby café, then used their bathroom to change out of her disguise. From her backpack she pulled out the one conservative outfit Shannon had packed for her, a dark gray, ankle-length skirt, black V-neck sweater with a gray rose appliquéd across the chest and a pair of ankle-high black leather boots. She put them on, combed her hair, applied lipstick and a little mascara. The picture of modesty and respectability, she decided as she checked her image in the mirror.

But she was nervous, she had to admit it. She wasn't quite sure just what she'd say to Peter Hausner. She would, of course, not mention the threats on her life, but she wanted the family lawyer to know of her existence, so she could find out more about her birth mother, get a sense of her genetic heritage. It seemed a reasonable quest to her.

And if in some part of her brain she wished JR were there, to come up with the right questions, to be able to talk to another lawyer in that special language they all had, well, then, she'd just have to do the best she could on her own. It was becoming more and more obvious to her how much she'd grown to depend on JR and how little he trusted her to take care of herself. Their recent phone conversation had proved it.

The offices were decorated with pale wood paneling and richly upholstered couches; the artwork on the walls was signed and numbered. The receptionist, according to the nameplate on her highly polished antique desk, was Gwendolyn Payne. She was about Carmen's own age, and there the similarity ended. She was perfectly groomed and made-up, in an ivory silk blouse with pearl buttons, little pearls in her ears, straight, dark hair worn shoulder length and not a strand out of place. It was a look, she was starting to realize, she probably would never be able to pull off.

"Hi," she said, with determined cheer. "My name is Coyle, Goldie Coyle, actually, but everyone calls me Carmen."

"And what may I do for you, Ms. Coyle?"

"I'm wondering if Mr. Hausner is free."

"Do you have an appointment?"

"No, I don't."

The perfectly painted mouth turned down at the corners. "I'm sorry, but Mr. Hausner is quite busy, Ms. Coyle. May I set you up with something for the end of the week? Perhaps," she went on, perusing the screen on her computer, "on Friday? Say, at eleven?"

Carmen scrunched up her nose. "I'm sorry. I don't live here in Scottsdale. I'm only in town for the day. And there's some personal business I need to discuss with him. It concerns the Kurtz estate."

Pursing her lips in disapproval, she picked up a phone. "Sorry to bother you, Mr. Hausner," the receptionist said in a beautifully modulated voice, "but there's a Ms. Coyle here and she'd like to see you. She says it has to do with the Kurtz estate and that it's confidential."

She listened for a few moments, then nodded. "Yes, I told her you were busy.... Yes, I did.....". The frown again, followed by, "Well, all right. If you say so." She hung up and said stiffly, "Mr. Hausner says if you'll wait, he can give you ten minutes in about a half hour or so."

Carmen settled herself in a chair and read the latest showbiz magazine, getting about a lifetime's fill of the most recent divorces, face-lifts, awards and visits to drug rehabs, not to mention the latest round of celebrity adoptions of Third World orphans, who were not only dragged across continents to be fussed over and posed for photographs with their famous celebrity moms, but were also given names such as Orange, Kong and Delphinium. Poor babies.

Of course, someone had named *her* Goldie Raquel. Both of them movie star names from the previous generation. She needed to ask Mom whose idea that was, because she wasn't particularly nuts about either name.

"Ms. Coyle?" At the sound of a deep male voice, she looked up.

The gray-haired, rather portly, middle-aged man with an expensive suit and haircut was not tall, maybe five-eight or so. When Carmen stood and offered her hand, they were at eye level. "Mr. Hausner?"

As he shook her hand, then quickly dropped it, his expression was pleasant, if not exactly welcoming. "Come back to my office. Gwen, hold my calls for just a few moments."

Hausner's office was quietly tasteful and nonostentatious, filled with antiques. A wide window let in soft Arizona light. He sat behind his uncluttered desk, indicating she should sit in an upholstered chair, facing him.

He didn't offer coffee or any kind of refreshment. Instead, he glanced at his watch, as though to remind her of the ten-minute limit he had agreed on, and said, "This is about the Kurtz estate?"

"Yes."

"And what is your connection?"

She'd rehearsed this speech earlier. "Mr. Hausner," she began with a smile, "this is going to sound strange, but I ask your indulgence."

The jangling salsa music of her cell phone interrupted the moment. Hausner frowned as she frantically searched her backpack for the phone. When she found it she flipped it open. "Yes?"

"Carmen, I—"

"I can't talk now, JR. I'll call you later."

Turning off the ringer so this wouldn't happen again, she closed the phone, returned it to her backpack and offered an apologetic smile to the lawyer. "I'm so sorry. Now, where was I?"

"Asking my indulgence."

She nodded. "Just two days ago, I found out something startling, having to do with my birth. The woman I call my mother is not actually my biological mother. I was born to a woman named Phoebe Kurtz. She died shortly after I was born." She watched his face for any reactions, but he had his show-nothing, keep-your-lawyerly-distance mask on; she'd seen both JR and Shannon use it, and Hausner was as good as they were. "Are you aware of any of this?"

Instead of answering her question, he studied her smilelessly for a moment or two, then said, "May I ask the nature of your inquiry?"

"I just told you."

He rested his elbows on his desk and steepled his fingers. "No, I mean, what do you hope to accomplish by coming here today and telling me this?"

"Accomplish? Nothing. I mean, I don't really know." She smiled again, inviting him to understand how earth-shaking the recent news had been for her. "I just found out and it took me totally by surprise. So I thought, well, that I'd come here and—" she shrugged "—maybe visit with my grandfather, find out if there are any other relatives, you know, ask some questions about what Phoebe was like. Maybe even get some names of her friends. Get a picture of just who she was. As I'm sure you can imagine, it's kind of strange. Finding out that one half of your genetic makeup was inherited from someone you had no idea existed until yesterday. Anyhow, I thought I'd start with you. And that's why I'm here."

She smiled again, encouraging him to smile back.

Instead, he studied her some more, this time through half-lidded eyes. Although he kept his expression un-readable, she had the sense that he was having a reaction. A pretty strong one.

Her intuition was validated when he finally rose, walked to his office door and opened it. "I'll ask you to leave now, Ms. Coyle."

"Excuse me?"

"Please, Ms. Coyle." Now the disdain was obvious. "As anyone who is anyone in Scottsdale knows, Hiram Kurtz is a very wealthy man. He worked hard and long to achieve his wealth, beginning as a lowly gardener and winding up owning gardening and home improvement centers all over the Southwest. He is an admirable man, a respected man, a pillar of the community. Hiram Kurtz is also a very old man, ill and incapacitated. My job is to protect him, from shock, from bad news—" he paused for emphasis "—and from fortune hunters. Now, either you are incredibly naive or incredibly skilled. Either way, I intend to look out for his best interests. That does not include answering your questions."

She remained seated, shocked by his cold, pointed comments. "But, I—"

He didn't allow her to finish her sentence. "Phoebe Kurtz is dead. If you are her daughter—and I doubt you are, as this is the first I've heard of your existence— please have your lawyer contact me. You may take one of my cards from the reception desk. Good day."

She stood, shaking her head. "But I didn't come here to—"

"Good day, Ms. Coyle." Once again he cut her off, dismissing her as though she were a gnat who had dared to breathe the same air as him.

Confused, smarting from unfounded accusations, Carmen headed for the door. But before exiting, she paused in the doorway as the healing rush of outrage took over. She looked him directly in the eye. "I'm not what you think I am, Mr. Hausner. I'm simply trying to connect with my family."

"I doubt that, Ms. Coyle."

He began to close the door, and if she hadn't jumped out of the way, might have slammed it into her back.

She glared at the now closed door, thought about heading right back in there and telling him off. How dare he? But caution took over, rare though that was for

Carmen. This was too important to risk blowing it. She needed to think this through before acting rashly.

Head held high, she walked down the corridor, past the reception desk—where she did *not* take one of his cards, thank you—and out into the hallway. Once there, she sagged against the wall.

What was that all about? she asked herself, even as echoes of Hausner's accusations whirled around in her head. *Incredibly naive or incredibly skilled…a fortune hunter…if you are Phoebe Kurtz's daughter*. Doubt as to her claims, doubt as to her motives.

She tried to summon the outrage again, but it had already lessened. In fact, she had to admit, had she been in charge of protecting a sick old man from the world, she might have had the same reaction as the lawyer.

But…a fortune hunter? That was so *not* who she was. The thought hadn't even crossed her mind that there might be an estate, that she might be entitled to part of the estate. It still wasn't crossing her mind. She was a Coyle, not a Kurtz. All she wanted were some answers—why had Phoebe been estranged from her family? Were any of them even aware she'd had a daughter? Was there anyone she could talk to about all this?

Could anyone come up with a reason someone wanted Carmen dead?

Was there anyone who cared?

JR. His face, his chiseled, dear face, flew into her head, making her smile at the picture. JR cared. And she cared about him. More even than before. Because they had slept together? Or because she was actually allowing herself to—she gave a mental gulp before she completed the thought—fall in love?

Was that it? Good heavens. Was she ready to face it and, as the expression went, to own it?

Oh, boy. She needed to let this little notion simmer for a while, she realized. Wait and see if it was real or just a lifeline she was grabbing on to at a moment in time when she needed one really badly.

Breathe in, breathe out. Breathe in, breathe out. Okay, then. What to do next about the Kurtzes? Of course. She would go to the source, visit the man who was her grandfather.

Or not. He was sick and old. Hausner said no one knew Phoebe had had a child, so Carmen's suddenly popping up might be too much for him. It might shock him, make him sicker.

At least now, though, she thought with another light-ning-quick mood swing, she had information that had been worth the trip to Arizona. New details that she'd obtained by herself and about herself: she was de-scended from gardeners! That's where she got her love of all green and growing things. She wasn't a Martian. She *belonged* somewhere.

Not, of course, that she didn't also belong to the Coyles—she was Gerald's daughter, too. But now she knew that there was a historical precedent for her green thumb.

Kurtz Nurseries, she thought happily, willing away the sour taste in her mouth left by Hausner and his ac-cusations. She would go visit Kurtz Nurseries, see what Hiram had created. Excited, she walked quickly out the door of the office building and was lucky enough to find a cruising taxi. "Do you know where the nearest Kurtz Nursery is?" she asked the cabbie when she got in.

"About three miles away."

"Take me there, please."

She glanced at her watch. Noon. Arizona, she'd learned, didn't observe daylight savings time so, at this time of year, Phoenix was in the same time zone as California. She owed JR a phone call.

"JR," she whispered as, again, she felt this lovely warmth fill her chest. He truly was a special man. *Was* she in love with him? Was this what love, real, grown-up, grow-old-together, love-with-a-capital-*L* felt like? But it didn't hurt. Wasn't love supposed to hurt?

She opened her cell and called his office, but his secretary said he wasn't back yet. She asked for his voice mail and when she got it said, "Hi, JR. It's me. I just got out of the lawyer's office. He wasn't too happy with me—thought I was some kind of fortune hunter. He said the family knew Phoebe was dead, but had never heard of my existence. But at least I found out that my biological mother's family were gardeners. Doesn't that explain a lot? I'm not sure if you understand, but that makes me feel so much better. Anyway, I'm not sure if I'm going to visit my grandfather, because he's pretty old and sick and I don't want to upset him. Maybe I'll contact him another day. For now, though, I'm going to check out a couple of the nurseries owned by the family. Kurtz Nurseries, that's what they're called."

She lowered her voice and whispered into the phone, "And listen…I just want you to know that…um, I'm thinking about you. Missing you, actually. A lot," she added. "Bye."

She snapped the phone closed and watched the scenery go by out the window, eager to stroll up and down long aisles bursting with shrubs and flowers, trees and herbs, all of it smelling of wet, dark, soil, mulch and fertilizer.

Eager to be where she felt totally at home.

Chapter 11

"**Y**ou really want to know why I didn't tell you all this before?" JR barked into the phone, aware he was raising his voice. Also that he was in his office and it wasn't the kind of thing the members of his firm usually did while speaking on the phone, but just not giving a damn. "You really want to know?"

"Yes, I do," Mac said evenly on the other end of the line. "Sunday morning I dropped in on you and your girlfriend at the hotel, remember? And gave you a resource? And asked you to let me know as soon as you found anything out? Remember?"

"Well, we've been kind of busy here, Detective." JR's temper was approaching the boiling point; he knew it and couldn't do a thing about turning down the burner. "Carmen found out Sunday afternoon that her mother wasn't her mother," he said through clenched teeth, "so then we hauled it up to Santa Barbara and got confirmation from the woman who raised her, and who Carmen always called her mother, even though she wasn't, biologically speaking, and then they had to work everything out, so we didn't get back till late last night." It was a run-on sentence worthy of Carmen herself, but he didn't care. "Then, early this morning, Carmen took off without telling me where she was going. Apparently, whatever watchdogs your captain provided managed to miss her as she left, as she was wearing a disguise."

Furious at Carmen, the police, the world in general all over again, JR walked over to the window and gazed out, seeing nothing. "I've been attending to business all morning for my *real* job, as opposed to my *volunteer* job of looking out for a woman whose life is in danger. My shoulder hurts like the blazes. I can't take pain meds because they knock me out and I can't function. No one seems to know what the hell is going on. I now know where Carmen is but am not sure if the bad guys have gotten to her yet. And your feelings are hurt because I didn't tell you sooner? Excuse me, Detective, but in the scheme of things, as far as priorities go, pardon me if I don't apologize. In fact, pardon me if I don't give a rat's ass!"

A long silence greeted his outburst, during which JR wondered if Mac had hung up and he'd been too filled with righteous fury to hear the disconnect. Then the detective spoke, his voice calm and measured. "You through, Counselor?" he said, sounding like a health care professional trying to talk down a jumper from the top of the building. "You feel better now? You done with your little tantrum?"

"Tantrum?"

"You got a better word? Fine, one day we'll play 'Can you top this synonym?', but for now, we got more pressing things to take care of."

JR had to admire Mac's refusal to engage him in a pissing contest. Because, of course, the detective was right. JR—who usually prided himself on his control—might be at the end of his rope, due to pain, lack of sleep, worry and the intrusion of his work life on his private life, but all that really didn't matter, not now. Carmen did.

He whooshed out a breath, then said, "I'm through. I do feel better, actually. And I apologize. I had no right to dump on you like that."

"Apology accepted. Now, you tell me what Ben's report said—the names, the details—and I'll take it from there."

When JR had finished reading Ben's findings to Mac, the detective said, "Got it. And you have no idea where Carmen is?"

"The last time she called me, about two hours ago, she'd just been to see the Kurtz family lawyer, who wasn't too pleased to see her."

"Name?"

"Peter Hausner. He's in Scottsdale. I just finished talking to Ben—apparently, Carmen went by this morning and got the name from him."

"Okay."

"After she saw the lawyer, she called me and said she was going to wander around some nurseries."

"Nurseries? Like babies?"

"No, plants. Carmen loves plants and flowers. She's got the most amazing green thumb—she's rescued every growing thing she's ever come in contact with." He could picture Carmen in the tiny garden she'd cultivated in the rear of her house, her oversize green watering can dispensing moisture as she chatted with her flowers. Always so tender, so solicitous, as though each plant had its own soul. Despite his present mood, he had to smile at the image, and he felt a slight easing in his chest.

"A pretty special lady," Mac observed, taking a little side trip from the main topic of discussion. "You two together, or what?"

The million-dollar question. "When I know I'll let you know."

"Like that, huh? Well, look, give her a call, let her know we're on it at this end."

"I tried. She isn't answering, so I left word on her voice mail. At least she cleared her messages."

"And this lawyer. Hausner? Let me nose around, see what I can come up with."

"You'll get back to me when you have something?" JR asked, then added ruefully, "Sooner than I got back to you?"

Mac's quiet chuckle was followed by, "Count on it, Counselor."

JR hung up the phone, drummed the fingers of his right hand on his desk, glanced at the files in his in-basket and then at his calendar. No contest, really—who was he kidding? He punched in the button that connected him to his secretary. Time to get a move on.

JR's cell phone rang while he was on the way to the airport.

It was Ben. "Look," he said, "I found something hinky about that lawyer for the Kurtz family."

JR was on full alert. "Go on."

"A while back, years ago, he conducted a search to find the missing daughter, Phoebe, right? And he told Carmen that he was unaware of her existence, right?"

"Right."

"Well, that's just bull. He knows all about Carmen, down to her name, address and social security number. It was all in the report he got."

JR didn't want to know how Ben got hold of what was obviously a confidential report. It was amazing how your normally ethical behavior flew right out the window when someone you loved was in danger. But right now, he had more important things to attend to: Hausner. The lawyer was dirty, he knew it in his gut, and his fears for Carmen's safety were back.

From his daily dealings with billion-dollar corporations, JR had found that whenever there was big money, there was a major chance of big corruption. The temptation was just too hard to resist.

"Good work, Ben. I'm on my way to see Mr. Hausner as we speak."

Kurtz Xeriscaping was the third and most out-of-the-ordinary Kurtz nursery Carmen had visited. It was stocked with plants and project ideas for a planet whose water supply was drying up. Not just cacti, but also new drought-resistant strains of manzanita and pyracantha, new compost and mulching techniques. As she walked up and down the aisles, Carmen was filled with enthusiasm. Idea after idea sprang to mind, not only for her own little garden, but also Mom's hedges, and certainly Shannon's new storefront office. Mom and Shannon kept forgetting to water—this low-hydration technique was made just for them.

As she headed down a new aisle to examine a coffeeberry shrub, a figure darted quickly around the next corner, disappearing immediately from sight. It not only took her by surprise, but it spooked her, so she stepped behind a row of tall bushes in pots. Was it the shooter? Had he or she followed her from L.A.?

But…she'd been so careful all day. The disguise, paying cash at the airport, watching her back every step of the way. No, she hadn't been followed from L.A. She was sure of it.

However…she could have been followed since arriving in town. That lawyer, Hausner, could have had her followed.

Was she being overly suspicious? Maybe yes, maybe no. She wanted to believe badly of him because she hadn't liked his treatment of her. But let's say she was right and he was following her, or, more likely, having her followed. Why?

To see where she went next, of course.

Again, why? Why did he need to keep tabs on her? Was he afraid she was going to visit her grandfather, maybe upset him? That made sense. Hausner had no way of knowing that Carmen had earlier decided *not* to pop in on the old man.

Or maybe Hausner wanted to keep her away from Hiram for less humane reasons. Maybe there was something he didn't want Carmen—or her grandfather—to know. Well, too bad. That decided her on the next part of her plan. She would go to her grandfather's house.

Walk around, for starters, check the place out. She was curious, had a right to be.

She glanced at her watch. Three in the afternoon. It would be dark soon. If she was going to see anything, she'd better do it now.

As soon as JR disembarked at Sky Harbor International Airport, he turned on his cell phone. It rang immediately.

"Where the hell have you been?" It was Mac. "I've been trying to get you for the past two hours."

"On a plane. I just landed in Phoenix. What do you have?"

"Some answers. I called a cop friend of mine in Scottsdale, Gary Florez. Got the lowdown on Hausner. Apparently he's always been rock-solid, respected, from an old Arizona family. However, he's gotten into some recent trouble with debt. He's a gambler, big-time. Kept it under wraps for years, but lately, it's gotten out of hand."

His gut had been right! "Which means he needs access to money."

"Lots of money, according to Florez. He's mortgaged to the hilt."

"And I'll just bet he manages several trusts for several well-to-do clients. And where better to get hold of money than by milking an estate he's in charge of?"

"Okay, it's a good theory," Mac said. "But that's all it is, for now."

"Yeah, but it fits. Carmen told me that the lawyer told her he had no idea of her existence. Your friend Ben says that's a crock, that Hausner conducted a search years ago and found out about Carmen's birth. But he kept Carmen's existence from the Kurtz family. Why?"

"Or maybe he didn't."

"Excuse me...?"

"Maybe they do know about her. Maybe they've stayed away from her, for whatever reason. Respecting her privacy. Or they didn't want to be reminded of her mother. Who knows?"

JR was nearly to the taxi stand now. "I like the first theory better. Suppose Carmen's a major beneficiary in the old man's will? What if there's a clause that if she predeceases him, the money goes to the lawyer? No," he amended quickly, "it wouldn't be set up that way. It would go to a charitable foundation whose purse strings are controlled by the lawyer."

"Access to money, lots of it, for sure," Mac said. "But only if Carmen—the potential monkey wrench to his plans—is out of the picture."

"Which might explain the attempt on her life." He paused and frowned. "But why now, Mac? Why, if he's known about her existence for years, go after her now? What's the catalyst?"

"Florez says he heard that Hausner had to go to moneylenders about a month ago. And that there's a payment due that he can't make."

"Crunch time." JR nodded. "He can't wait for the old man to die, especially if a new young heir shows up, with her own lawyers and accountants, so he has to act now. He's planning to use Kurtz's money to pay off the moneylenders, and it's time to get rid of the one potential obstacle to getting away with it."

"You have a devious mind, Counselor," Mac said.

"Reminds me of mine. It's pure speculation, of course. Nothing I can act on."

"But *I* can. I'm here. I have to find Carmen. And soon." Tension coiled in his gut as he realized if his and Mac's speculations were in any way on the money, the danger to Carmen's life was as great as ever.

"Tell you what," Mac said. "Florez owes me a favor or two. I'll give him Carmen's description, see if he and a couple of his buddies can canvas all the Kurtz nurseries, see where she's been and where she hasn't been yet."

"She may be in disguise, remember? And I have no idea what the disguise is."

"Oh, yeah. We'll do the best we can."

"You seem to have a lot of people who owe you favors." JR, slightly out of breath from walking so fast, nodded to the attendant in charge of putting passengers in taxis.

Mac chuckled. "Thirty years on the job, the favors add up, both ways."

"I'm heading over to Hausner's office."

"My take? You're better off heading over to the old man's place."

"To see if Carmen's there or she's been there. Of course. Good thinking," he said, climbing into the backseat of a cab. "I'm on my way."

As she watched the taxi drive off, Carmen wondered if she should have let it go. She was alone on a deserted road. No one had followed her here—she'd been checking pretty thoroughly. Or if they had followed her, they'd stopped doing so when the taxi turned onto Halley Drive. She hadn't seen another car for the past five minutes. Which only meant that if Hausner *had* sent someone to follow her, there had been no need to make that last turn. Halley Drive was where her grandfather lived.

So now the lawyer knew where she was. Big deal. She was allowed to go wherever she wanted to.

She gazed up at the huge iron gates that kept visitors away from the Kurtz home. Home? Estate was a better description. Through the gates she could see a long and winding tree-lined road. So long and so winding, the house itself wasn't visible. There was a buzzer she could push, off to the side. Should she? How would she announce herself? The old "confidential matters to discuss" thing? If she said she was Phoebe's daughter, would they believe her? Laugh at her? Call the police?

She was chewing her lip, trying to decide, when she heard the sound of a motor in the distance. Quickly, she darted behind one of the tall Italian cypresses that had been sculpted into a hedgerow on either side of the gate. A UPS truck came over the rise, slowed down and pulled up to the gate. The driver pushed the button and spoke into the talk box. Soon, the huge iron gate swung open and the truck barreled through. Without thinking, Carmen stepped from behind the hedge and went through also, immediately ducking behind a tree, so as not to be observed.

Was she crazy? What was she doing?

Just looking around, she told herself. Just looking at where her grandfather lived. Was this where her mother had been raised? Had her childhood been one of privilege? Why had she been estranged from her family? Carmen wanted to know, *had* to know. At this moment, finding out about her biological mother was the most important thing in the world.

She would march up this driveway, she decided, and knock on the door. She really didn't have to worry about her grandfather answering the door and giving him a huge shock, because this was the kind of place where the people who lived here didn't answer the door themselves. There would be a maid or a butler. Carmen would ask to speak to some person in charge, explain quietly and calmly who she was, and ask if it was possible to see her grandfather.

She came out from her hiding place and began to make her way up the driveway. There were trees everywhere, she noted with appreciation, and it reminded her of a school trip she'd made once to California's state capital. In the park that surrounded Sacramento's government buildings were trees from every one of the fifty states. With all the species she was observing today, she wouldn't be surprised if the same were true on the Kurtz estate.

The road curved and climbed at the same time, and she had no idea how long she would be walking before she got to the front door, but get there she would.

The taxi pulled to a halt. "Here we are, mister."

JR gazed out the window, saw gates, trees, a winding road. "Push the button. I'll talk to them." He hopped out of the taxi and when a muffled voice came over the loud-speaker, saying, "Yes?" he replied, "My name is Stanton Fitzgerald Ewing. I'm a lawyer from Los Angeles, and I need to see Mr. Kurtz on a matter of great urgency."

There was a momentary pause, then the disembodied voice said, "I'm sorry, but we don't have you on the list of expected visitors."

"That's because I wasn't expected. But this is urgent, please believe me."

"I'm sorry, but—"

"All right," he interrupted, aware that his tension was showing and trying to rein it in. "Just answer a question for me, please. Have you had a visitor in the past couple of hours or so? A young, blond woman? About five foot eight? Her name is Goldie Coyle, but she goes by the name of Carmen."

"No, there's been no one here by that name today."

"Oh." The wind went out of his sails. Where the hell was she? "I would still like to see Mr. Kurtz."

"I'm sorry. Mr. Kurtz isn't well, and he's resting. Good day." And with that, the person disconnected.

JR muttered a curse. The taxi driver leaned an elbow on the open window. "What do you want to do, sir?"

"I supposed I ought to—" He didn't finish the sentence because his cell phone rang. He looked at the readout, then flipped it open. "Carmen? Where are you?"

"JR. Listen." She was whispering. "I'm at my grandfather's. I know I shouldn't have done this, but—"

"No, you're not."

"Excuse me?"

"I just asked them if you were there, and you're not."

"I'm not where?"

"At your grandfather's."

"I'm confused," Carmen said, still whispering. Why was she whispering?

"That makes two of us." JR told himself to calm down. Carmen was all right. Nothing bad had happened to her. Yet. "Okay, let's start over. Where are you?"

"I just told you." She sounded impatient. "Outside my grandfather's house."

He looked around. "No, I am."

"You are what?"

"Outside your grandfather's house."

"Really?"

This was a nightmare, he thought wildly, of the Abbott and Costello "Who's On First" variety. "I mean I'm here at the Kurtz estate, outside the gate."

"Oh! Well, I'm on the *other* side of the gate, leaning up against a tree, talking to you. But, JR, why are you here?"

"I came after you. I was worried."

"You're doing it again," she said, her tone of voice no longer conversational but displeased. "Taking care of me. JR, you have to stop this."

"But, Carmen, listen—"

"No, you listen. I was calling to let you know what I'm doing because you were so upset with me earlier. And now I find out you're *shadowing* me. You don't trust me at all, do you? This just isn't okay, JR. Really, it isn't." With that, she hung up.

He pressed Callback. The phone rang three times, and then, once again, he was switched over to voice mail. She was ignoring him or she had the ringer off. And this time, uttering a string of curses, he did throw the phone, against the gate. The movement made his injured shoulder ache, and he muttered another curse.

The taxi driver, who had been watching JR conduct his conversation with studied indifference, said, again, "What do you want to do, sir?"

JR took out some bills and thrust them at him. "Thanks."

"You don't want a ride? To somewhere else?"

"No, I'm fine."

The driver lifted his shoulders in a whatever-you-say shrug, backed up and drove off.

JR retrieved his cell phone, which, thank God, still worked, and called Mac.

"Marshall here."

"Oh, good. Listen. I found Carmen. She's okay. So far. She's about to knock on Kurtz's front door." As he spoke he surveyed the wall of ten-foot-high, smooth iron spikes. No footholds, nothing to grab on to. "I'm going to try to stop her. Or go in with her."

"Good move."

"Anything new with Hausner?"

"Working on it."

"Fine. Talk to you soon."

He hung up, then gazed up and down the long expanse of railing. Several yards to his left was a stand of tall trees, their branches drooping onto both sides of the fence.

Many years ago, Carmen had been the one to show a skinny, secretly asthmatic kid with thick glasses how to climb trees. In the years that followed, he'd become rather good at it, even if he did say so himself. One of his arms was nearly useless, of course, but he still had one good one and two strong legs.

He'd never broken into and entered private property before, but there was always a first time.

"First he tells me to grow up and take responsibility," Carmen muttered to herself, "then he tails me like I'm some kind of runaway teenager."

The UPS truck passed her going the other way as she continued marching up the winding path.

Shannon was right. It took two. If Carmen had leaned

too much on JR all these years, he'd welcomed it—
some part of him got off on her needing him so much.
JR was a real caretaker type, just like Shannon said.

Well, she didn't need taking care of. Didn't need a
keeper.

It must have been at least a mile, but finally she
rounded a bend and saw it. A huge stone house. She
stopped and stared, her mouth open. Wow. It was like
some member of the British royalty's alternate palace.
Three stories high, with turrets and chimneys and all
kinds of wood-framed windows. Not new, either. Not
one of those pompous McMansions causing gentrifica-
tion meltdown all over L.A. No, this house was classic
and classy, truly awe-inspiring.

Her appreciation was interrupted by a faint droning
sound from behind her, and at first she thought it was
some kind of insect. As the noise grew louder she glanced
back over her shoulder to see a large black car barreling
up the road. Whoever was driving sure seemed to be in
a hurry. She stepped to the side of the road to let them
pass, but the strangest thing happened. As the car—a
Mercedes, she could see now—drew nearer, it swerved
sharply to the right, seemingly headed right at her.

For a moment, she stood right where she was, frozen
in shock. The car was closing in, but she finally woke
up, turned around and began to run. She'd waited just
a little too long, though. The car was right there, practically on top of her. Suddenly something, someone,
tackled her, pushing her over to the side, temporarily out
of harm's way.

It was a déjà vu kind of thing, just like what had
happened at the beach on Friday. As he had then, it was

JR who was doing the tackling, the rolling her over and over, away from the road, deeper into the woods.

But today, when they stopped rolling, she heard a loud "Oof!" in her ear. She disentangled herself from JR and looked at him as he lay there, on the ground, clutching his shoulder in agony.

"Oh, no!" Her first instinct was to tend to him, but the sound of a slamming car door brought her right back to the immediate danger at hand. She looked up to see Peter Hausner coming around the rear of the car, apparently not sure whether he'd hit his target.

Her.

As soon as his gaze locked on hers, his eyes widened. Then he sprinted back toward the driver's door. That was Carmen's cue. Enraged, she leaped up and ran toward the black automobile, making it to the passenger side door and yanking it open just as Hausner took off again. Grabbing the headrest for support, she scrambled onto the seat.

As he realized she was now in the car, Hausner—who was bent over the steering wheel like a mad scientist, a fierce, crazed look on his face—let out a cry of rage and aimed the car for the area where JR lay.

Carmen screamed back and launched herself at him, grabbing the steering wheel and yanking it to the left, away from JR. As they fought over the wheel, the car kept bucking and inching forward, first to the right, then to the left.

The lawyer was older and fatter than Carmen, and she was in pretty good shape, so she figured she had the advantage. She also had nails. When he managed to pry her fingers off the steering wheel, she went for his eyes, scratching him for all she was worth. He howled in protest, releasing the steering wheel to fend her off. Still using her left hand to push at and damage his face as much as she could, Carmen managed to use her right to pull up the emergency parking brake. The car shuddered to a screeching halt. She leaned an elbow on the horn, keeping it there, trying to signal anyone within hearing distance.

Hausner fought her, hard. But now that she knew *he* had to be the monster behind all the recent events, she had raw, hot fury on her side. Rage for poor Peg Davis, rage at having been the target of an assassin, rage for JR's wounded shoulder, rage at being nearly run over. She got onto her knees, screamed epithets at him, raked her fingernails over his face, kneed him in the abdomen, would have kneed him in the groin if the angle had been right.

Finally he gave up fighting. He reached behind him for the door handle, got it open and tumbled out of the car. He scrambled to his feet and took off, heading toward the side of the house. Carmen slid into the driver's seat, released the brake and tried to restart the engine, fully intending to run him down. The car refused to start—too many mixed messages in the past few moments, probably, but, whatever, it was dead.

Leaning on the horn again, she watched Hausner disappear around the side of the house and head for the woods beyond.

Then she remembered. JR! She leaped out of the car and ran over to where he lay, clutching his shoulder, obviously in pain but gritting his teeth against it. As she knelt beside him, she heard the sound of sirens in the distance. Whew!

"Are you all right?" she asked JR, barely able to get the words out, she was panting so hard with exertion.

He, too, was having trouble catching his breath. "Damn shoulder. I think the stitches tore open. You okay, Carm?"

"I'm great." Even though her chest was heaving and she was having trouble catching her breath. And her face hurt from where Hausner had scratched and punched her.

"Where is he? Hausner?"

"He took off into the woods." She really couldn't sit up anymore, so she plopped down on her back next to JR. Overhead, a huge, spreading black oak tree blocked out whatever was left of daylight.

"The cops are on the way," Carmen managed between gasps. "I think. There are sirens."

"Mac's friend must've called them. He's been on it."

"Good ol' Mac."

JR's shoulder felt as though someone had set fire to it. But he could deal with that later, he figured. Carmen was safe, help was on the way. That was all that mattered. The sirens grew louder, his breathing got easier.

He turned his head to the side. She lay there, chest heaving, eyes closed, scratches all over her, a bad bruise on her cheek. "Carm. You saved my life," he said, his voice cracking with dryness…not to mention emotion.

"And you saved mine," she replied. "Twice, actually. But who's counting?" She turned her head, locked gazes with him and grinned.

He smiled back. "I wasn't following you, Carm. Well, I was, but I was trying to warn you. Hausner was behind the whole thing."

"Yeah, I guessed that."

"When?"

"Just now, when he tried to run me down."

He chuckled, then had to stifle it. Any movement set off major shoulder pain. "How did you get him to take off like that?"

"Sheer fury. I've never felt like that before, JR," she said with wonder. "I would have killed him if I could."

"Wow." He took in another couple of breaths before saying, "Remind me never to piss you off."

"Consider yourself warned."

After that, all hell broke loose.

Later, after several patrol cars had screamed up the driveway, and a team of police officers had taken off after Hausner; after medical technicians had tended to both Carmen and JR; after Hausner had been hunted down, trying to scale an iron fence that couldn't be scaled without mountain-climbing equipment; after the lawyer had been handcuffed and taken away while Carmen and JR's statements were being taken by Mac's friend, Detective Florez; after JR and Carmen had been told to sit on a stone bench under one of the many trees surrounding the house and wait for Florez to finish up talking to whomever he'd contacted inside...

After all that, the front door of the Kurtz home opened. Through it came a frail old man in a wheelchair being pushed by a woman in late middle age with short, stylish blond hair. The two of them stood on the massive porch and peered into the distance.

"Excuse me," Carmen said to JR. "I...need to say hello."

She stood, nervously brushing off her skirt before walking slowly toward the house. When she was a few feet from the porch she stopped, as though waiting for instructions on what to do next.

The old man peered into the distance and when he set eyes on her, said, in a quivering voice, "Phoebe?"

The woman behind him put a hand to her mouth, then shook her head. "No, Dad," she said, loud enough for JR to hear her from his bench. "It's not Phoebe," the woman went on, the volume of her voice higher than normal, the way one spoke to the hard of hearing. "I'm pretty sure it's her daughter."

After patting the old man on the shoulder, the woman walked out from behind the wheelchair, came down the steps of the porch, and headed for Carmen, her hands outstretched.

"I'm your Aunt Barbara," she said. "And I'm so glad you've come."

Chapter 12

Carmen came breezing into the waiting room of the Scottsdale police station, where she and JR had agreed to meet after her initial visit with the Kurtzes and his to the emergency room to repair his stitches. When she saw him, she grinned and walked over to him. "Hey, JR. How's the shoulder?"

Still a little woozy from another dose of pain meds, he looked for signs of strain or sadness on her face but, despite a couple of Band-Aids and that bruise on her cheek, she seemed to glow. "Okay. How did everything go?"

"Great. Really. My aunt and my grandfather were very nice. Do you know what that piece of scum Hausner did? He did tell them of my existence, but lied to them and said I wanted no contact with them."

JR shook his head. "The guy's a real piece of work."

"Has he talked yet?"

"No, he's all lawyered up, as expected. But he's behind bars and with murder charges pending, he won't get out on bail. He'll probably talk eventually—they'll make him a deal."

"Oh, I see."

"Are you sure you're okay?" he asked her. "This has been a lot for you to take in."

She gazed at him for a moment, the frown between her brows deepening, then said, "You know something, JR? You really do have to stop worrying about me so much, feeling so responsible for me."

"I guess it's become a habit."

She nodded. "And it isn't all your fault, of course. I mean, I know I don't act very mature sometimes. But, well, I *have* managed to get through nearly thirty years of life, somehow. I'll never be as organized and sensible as you are, and I'll probably never do things the way you do them, but I'm doing the best I can, JR. And really, it would be better for both of us if you stopped thinking of me as someone who needs constant looking-after. I have to find my own way. I mean, I had a father, a wonderful one, and I don't need you to take his place."

By the end of her speech, he felt as though he'd been sucker punched. Everything she'd said was the truth, of course; he'd had the same thoughts himself. Still…

"I see," he said slowly. "So, what exactly are you saying? It sounds like you're breaking up with me." He tried to smile, as though he were kidding, but he didn't think it came out that way. "And we've barely gotten started."

She studied him for a few silent moments before nodding. "You know, in a way, I am breaking up with you. The old Carmen and the old JR need to say goodbye to each other."

"But I love you." It just burst out of him.

"Oh, JR. I love you, too."

"Do you?"

She nodded. "Yes. You were right, of course, even though I didn't like you telling me how I was feeling. I am in love with you."

Elation flowed through him. "Oh, Carm." He reached for her but she held up a hand.

"No, don't. See, I think that the best kind of love should be between two equals, and we're not. Equal, I mean. I depend on you too much. When I'm with you, I fall back into that old pattern of leaning on you, of finding my strength in you. It's what Mom would call dysfunctional."

"Patterns can change," he said.

"Not easily."

"No, you're right. But they can."

She gazed at him, studying his face for something, but he didn't know what it was. Finally, she sighed. "Look, you need to get back, I know you do. I've been invited to hang around for a few days, get to know my grandfather and my aunt, meet the rest of the family."

Another sucker punch, but he tried to hide it with a smile. "Just as long as you come back. To L.A.," he said lightly.

Just as long as you come back to me, was what he'd nearly said, but had stopped himself just in time. She would perceive it as an "order."

He was confused. Carmen was in love with him. This was good, really good, news. But at the same time, she seemed to be pulling away from him. Not so good.

His confusion must have showed on his face—or maybe she just intuited it—after all, they'd known each other a long time—because her next words were, "Give me time. Okay?"

So it wasn't over. Yet. There was hope. Some, anyway. She loved him. He would keep that thought, fan that flame instead of giving in to despair. "Sure," he said. "Take some time." He gave a rueful chuckle. "Hell, I've been waiting for you for twenty years. I guess I can wait a few days longer."

With that, he used his good arm to pull her close, then he kissed her.

Intent on imprinting himself on her sensual memory, he made it a deep, sexy kiss, running his tongue along her upper and lower lips before thrusting it into her mouth to meet hers. He was pleased to hear her response, a soft, throaty moan. There, he thought, drawing back. Her eyes were glazed with surprise and passion, just as he'd wanted. She wouldn't forget him that easily now.

"See you soon, Carm," he said, then gave her a jaunty smile and headed for the station door and the airplane home.

Thanksgiving smells had to be the best smells ever, Carmen thought as she gazed out the kitchen window that overlooked the driveway.

"Shane Coyle," she heard her mother say behind her, "don't you dare take another bite of that stuffing or there'll be nothing left for the rest of us."

"But, Mom…"

Carmen had to smile. It was the same whine she'd

heard from her younger brother her entire life. "But, Mom…" He was twenty-four now, six foot two, had women draped over him wherever he went, had all kinds of firms bidding for his services after he finished up his Ph.D., but he still sounded like a five-year-old. "But, Mom…"

"Hey," Shannon said, walking up to stand next to her. "Why do you keep looking out the window?"

"She's waiting for JR," Grace said.

"Thought so. That's why you've been pacing like a caged lion for the past two hours."

"I have not been pacing like a caged lion. I've been very busy making cranberry relish and the sweet potato thingie I make every year to even think about pacing."

"You've been pacing mentally."

"Shannon," Grace chided. "Leave your sister alone."

Shannon turned around to face her mother. "Excuse me? You've seen her. She's about to jump out of her skin."

"Yes, I have, and she doesn't need you to tell her what she's feeling. Shane? I warned you."

"But, Mom…"

Carmen and Shannon looked at each other and laughed. Then Carmen put her arm around her much smaller sibling and hugged her.

Life was good. She'd returned from the Kurtzes earlier in the week, had taken care of some stuff at her place, then headed up here. She and Mom and Shannon—and Shane, after his arrival from the East Coast—had had talks about the family secret…good talks. Nothing had changed, really. She was still Carmen Coyle. It was just that there were now more family members in her life. As far as Carmen was concerned, you could never have enough family.

"Hey, Carm. Guess what?" Shannon said. "Your friend Mac? When he retires at the end of the year, he's going to pitch in at the storefront."

"That's great."

She only heard Shannon with half her brain. The other half was, indeed, on JR. They'd spoken briefly since her return, when she'd invited him up to Santa Barbara for Thanksgiving. He'd been snowed under with work, he'd told her, and looked forward to seeing her.

"Well, look who's here," Shannon said.

A car was coming up the driveway. It was JR's Lexus. Carmen's heart began to flutter wildly. She had so much to tell him!

She flew out of the back door and ran down the driveway. As soon as he opened the car door, she hugged him, tight.

He laughed. "Now that's what I call a greeting."

"Oh, JR, how I've missed you."

His blue eyes, behind his gold-rimmed glasses, were warm. "Me, too, Carm."

JR took in the pretty dress Carmen wore today, all browns and oranges and other autumn hues, but mostly he let his gaze feast on her face. Her bruises were mostly healed, her eyes were shining, her hair was clean and combed. She'd even put on some lipstick. None of which she needed to be beautiful to him. Still and always.

He reached into his car and pulled out a bag filled with several bottles of good wine. "Mom and Dad send their love. They decided to extend their cruise, but they'll see us at Christmas."

"Good." Her eyes were shining as she smiled at him.

Shane, Shannon and Grace all came out of the house at once, the women hugging JR and Shane shaking his hand. Carmen handed her brother the bag filled with wine. "Take this in, will you, squirt?" She put her arm through JR's bent elbow. "See you soon, everyone," she called out. "My best friend and I are going for a little walk."

Grace put a shawl around Carmen's shoulders. "It's chilly. You'll catch a cold."

"Once a mother…" she said, which earned a laugh from Grace.

My best friend.

JR repeated the phrase silently. She'd called him her best friend. Had she said that on purpose? Was that all that was behind her warm greeting? Was that all they were to each other? Was that all they were destined to be to each other?

They strolled down a familiar dirt path that ran behind the house and led into the woods. "I have so much to tell you, JR," she said, looking up at him with those bright eyes. "But first, before I start blabbing away, tell me how you are."

"Nothing major, Carm. I won a case, another one settled. I played racquetball. I saw a movie. And I thought about you. A lot. Now, talk. I want to hear everything."

She let out a sigh. "Oh, JR. I finally know what I'm supposed to be doing with my life. I had some hints before but I didn't know how to make a living from, you know, plants, so they were always a hobby. Well, forget that. It's not my hobby anymore, it's my calling."

"Good, Carm. It's the right thing."

She squeezed his arm. "I knew you'd approve. My

grandfather approved for sure. And my Aunt Barbara—
boy, can that woman cry! Buckets and buckets. She'd
always loved Phoebe, you see. Barbara was the older
sister, the 'good daughter,' and Phoebe was always
getting into trouble. By the way, I'm named after two
of Phoebe's favorite movie stars—Goldie Hawn and
Raquel Welch. Anyhow, Barbara needed to talk about
her, which was fine with me, of course. So I just sat and
listened. It felt so healing, JR. For all of us, really, but
they were so sad, and then we talked and I could see
them cheering up, especially my grandfather. Actually,
I don't think of him as my grandfather, not really,
because let's face it, all I know is the Coyle family and
Mom's family, the Goodes. But you know."

God, how he'd missed her! Missed her happy chatter,
missed the way she hopped from one topic to another, but
usually made it back to the starting line with that logic that
was purely Carmen's and nobody else's he'd ever met.

"They have a new lawyer," she went on, "and he's
much nicer. He said I needed to hire my own lawyer
because I have a claim on the estate, and I said I really
didn't want anything and then my aunt said of course I
did and that there was plenty to go around, even after
Peter Hausner dipped into it. And then I was embarrassed because they were talking about money, so I
started picking at the dead leaves on the philodendron
that was on the coffee table—the poor thing was just
starved for some minerals—and Barbara said, 'Oh, my
heavens, Phoebe used to do the same thing, take care of
my plants.' And then she cried some more."

JR had to chuckle. "Too many tears for me."

She grinned up at him and nodded. "It was definitely

damp out. And that's when I told them about how much
flowers and plants mean to me. And then we got to
talking some more. Well, actually, all this happened
over a period of a few days. Barbara said maybe it was
a blessing that I showed up when I did because Hiram
is so old now and no one else in the family really cared
anymore. About plants, I mean. That maybe we could
talk about me taking over some of the business. At
which point, I interrupted to say that, sorry, I have absolutely no head for business. Also that they were being
very generous but that it was way too much and way too
soon. But then I thought about it, and I told them the
truth, which is usually the best way to go, right?"

"Right."

A breeze came up as they walked along, rattling the
leaves on a tree they were passing, and bringing with it
the smell of the nearby ocean.

"I told them I wasn't there to rob anyone or sue anyone
for an inheritance. But that I would like a career and I'd
like it to involve being around a plant nursery, and
Barbara said they were expanding to Southern California, and I said maybe I could, you know, apprentice and
learn the business from the ground up, even though, as
I'd said, I don't have a head for business. And she waved
me away and said, 'Silly, neither do I, neither does
Hiram, that's what lawyers and accountants are for.'"

She grinned happily. "See?"

God, he loved her! "Yes, I see."

"And so I'm going to take a couple of night courses
at Santa Monica College. You know, small business
stuff and how to become more computer savvy. If I have
trouble I'll get a tutor to help. But you know, I don't

think I'm going to need help. I always had trouble in school because my mind was buzzing so loudly with all these voices telling me I couldn't do it, wasn't up to it, didn't have the brains the rest of my family had. It was so noisy in there I couldn't concentrate. And, now, if I don't have those voices—"

She stopped dead in her tracks and gazed up at him, brown eyes wide and very serious. "Not that I hear voices, JR. I mean, I'm not saying that."

He smiled, kissed her quickly on the nose. "I know you don't. Go on."

They resumed walking. A bird chattered on a high branch; another answered.

"It's that buzz of self-defeat," Carmen said. "That's what those voices are. And, boy, does it get in the way. But I don't feel that way now, so...down on myself. Something about these past few weeks has changed me. I'm still a Coyle and I still love and cherish my family. But I found out where I come from, or half of me, anyway, and back there, with the Kurtzes, I'm not an oddball. It's, well, it's just comforting. Barbara said Phoebe was just like me—isn't that interesting? Not great in school, but basically smart and really gifted with flowers. I saw pictures of her and actually I look more like Dad, but there is some resemblance.

"From what I could tell, the estrangement from the family had to do with the expectations everyone placed on her—she was to go to the 'right' college and marry the 'right' man, take her place in that upper-crust Scottsdale society. Big expectations, big plans, without consulting her. So she ran away.

"And poor Hiram. As he got older, he knew he'd

made a big mistake. And they tried to find her and they got Hausner on it and he reported to them that she'd died, but left out the part about me being born. At first. Later on, well, I already told you. What a piece of turd. He's the kind that makes people hate lawyers, which isn't fair. Not really."

"But it makes for some pretty funny lawyer jokes."

She grinned up at him again. "That it does. Okay if we keep walking? I have a lot of energy today."

"So I've noticed. And walking's fine."

JR knew Carmen very well, as she did him, and, yes, she had a lot to catch him up on, but this veritable cascade of verbiage also meant that she was in avoidance mode. It was one of her patterns—pacing instead of dealing, speed-talking instead of confronting. Was she avoiding talking about the two of them?

He'd been doing some thinking of his own on the topic. A lot of it. He could bring the subject up, he supposed. Force her to talk about it now, rather than later. But he was reminded of what she'd said back at the Scottsdale police station: she operated differently than he did. She had her own ways of dealing with life and he needed to accept her rather than try to change her. Not an easy proposition, for him, for most people.

While he'd been musing, Carmen had been chatting away, and he'd lost track. "I'm sorry, Carm," he told her, "go back to what you were saying about Hausner. Did they finally get him to talk?"

"Yes. Just like you said, he made a deal. Reduced charges and so on. But lots of jail time. And at least we got the whole story. It was just like you and Mac thought. Hausner kept the knowledge of my existence to himself. Then he got into trouble with the gambling. Especially with all the Native American casinos around—he used to have to travel, you know, go somewhere else, to Vegas or Reno whenever he could. But now, it was practically next door.

"And so he began to siphon off money from the estate, not just from the Kurtzes, although they were the biggies. And every time he stole money, he worried about me and my existence more and more. What if I showed up one day and put in my claim? What if I wasn't so easy to fool as the rest of them? And then he had a really bad night at the tables and he couldn't siphon off enough money in time, so he went to the moneylenders. You know, the kind of guys who break arms for a living."

"Bad move."

"He'd stopped being rational. He needed to keep Hiram alive and needed me dead. That was the equation he came up with. Just until he could win all the money back on the tables. You know, the way they always think they're going to, one day." She shook her head at the stupidity of gamblers' illusions. "So he hired a killer. And, by the way, not a top-notch killer—he didn't have the money for that, can you believe it? He got one who didn't cost as much. Isn't that *insane?* I mean, discounted killers. Like there's a coupon or something, fifteen percent off."

JR laughed, and Carmen looked up at him and laughed with him. "Silly, huh."

Oh, that joy-filled smile. How he'd missed it. "Extremely silly. Go on."

"So this killer—Mac's friend, Detective Florez, said

he was some assassin in training, someone's nephew—he followed me from home on the day I went to Nordstrom, watched me buy the sandals, followed me up the escalator, hung around while I went into the dressing room and then shot poor Peg Davis. And, yeah, it was a him not a her, by the way. Anyhow, he tried to break into my place the next night. He'd been told to search for papers, you know, to check and see if I was even aware of Phoebe's existence."

"We talked about that, remember? The night we were throwing ideas back and forth?"

"You were right. Anyhow, two days later, the nephew person found out that I wasn't dead, which must have bummed him out big-time, so he kept tabs on my place, but I didn't show up there—I was at your place, remember? Or Shannon's. It's hard to keep all the places I've been these past couple of weeks straight in my head."

"Such a pretty head," he said, stopping and bringing her hand up to his mouth and kissing it. He watched the color rise on her cheeks. Good. She was still attracted to him; that amazing sizzle they'd shared for one night was still in the air.

She ducked her head and they resumed walking. And Carmen resumed talking. "So he went to the funeral hoping I'd show up there, which I did. But there were cops around, so he waited and he trailed me to the beach with you. And tried again. Nearly made it, too." Her hand flew to her mouth. "Oh, I forgot. You don't have your sling on anymore. How's your shoulder?"

"Just fine. Go on."

"Really?"

"Promise. It's all better. Go on."

"Okay. So Hausner, hearing how once again this stupid hired assassin failed, called him off. The kid was making all these mistakes and he was terrified that this doofus would be traced back to him. So he kind of put off dealing with the problem of my existence and was just, I don't know, hoping it would all go away—talk about denial, huh? And then I show up in his office and he knows it's all over. He's done for."

She shook her head and frowned. "I gotta say, JR, I didn't get a whiff of this when I first met him. I mean, the man was good. Poker-faced, outraged at this intruder trying to pass herself off as an heir to the Kurtz fortune. Boy, I didn't pick up on a thing—no panic, nothing. Although it was kind of a tip-off when he practically slammed the door on my back that he was not entirely in control. And the fact that he agreed to see me without an appointment. I mean, you lawyers don't do that, do you?"

"Not often."

"So then he called someone the minute I left his office and told them to follow me. I kind of sensed that, but whoever it was, was pretty good because I never even saw anyone. I'm kind of new at this being followed thing. Not very good at it."

"May you never have to be good at it, ever."

"Amen. So then whoever was following me called Hausner and told him where I was and he ran out of his office, jumped in his car, thinking to warn the Kurtzes about me, that I was some imposter pretending to be Phoebe's daughter, stuff like that. And then he saw me walking up the driveway and he lost it, just lost it. His lawyer is suggesting he be charged with temporary insanity on that particular charge, which, of course, is not going to do him much good as he's already been indicted for Peg Davis's murder and attempted murder. Of me."

They'd arrived at an ancient tree whose gnarled roots were above ground, affording ample, and familiar, seating area. The two of them had taken many a stroll in these woods over the past four years, and had talked under this very tree. Now Carmen plopped down on one of the roots, emitting a loud sigh as she spread her hands. "So that's it. That's what happened. End of walk, end of story. All questions answered."

JR lowered himself onto the perch right next to hers. Taking a moment to gather his thoughts, he gazed up through the tree limbs at the sunshine. Dappled leaves, quiet. Birds chirping. Leaves rustling.

"May I ask you a question?" he said finally.

"Sure."

"Are we still friends?" He held his breath waiting for her answer.

Which she did not offer right away, which made his heart begin to sink slowly down toward his toes. She avoided his eyes, instead picking up a stick and tracing patterns in the dirt between them.

At last she said, "Well, now, that's kind of a problem." She kept her gaze averted, busy with her dirt patterns.

"Why is it a problem?"

She shrugged. "Well, see, the thing is—" she looked up briefly, then right back down again "—I still love you."

"And I still love you."

"No, I mean I still—" eyes up again "—love you."

Down again. More patterns now. Circles. "You know. The other kind. What I told you. Back in Scottsdale."

His heart, halted on its journey down to its toes, now soared upward, landing somewhere in the back of his throat. "You do?" He nearly couldn't get the words out.

"Yeah. And so, I wanted you to know that. Before."

Uh-oh. "Before what?"

As though deciding that avoidance no longer worked, Carmen brought her knees to her chest and wrapped her arms around them. She looked right at him. "Remember what I said about us not being equals? Well, I think I was right when I said it, but so much has gone down since then. I know where I want to go in life, what I want as my career. Did you know that there is a whole science devoted to low hydration and that Kurtz nurseries was a pioneer in the field?"

"No, I didn't," he said quietly. Waiting. She would get there, wherever "there" was, in her own time, on her own terms.

"The thing is, I like myself better, JR. There's more work to be done. I might get myself a little therapy— Mom thinks it would be a good idea and she should know. But I feel like, well, kind of a grown-up for the first time in my life. See, it turns out that I am going to inherit part of Hiram's empire. He insists on it, Barbara insists on it and hey, I'm not stupid. I mean, I want him to live forever, but it's not going to happen. So I'm going to come into some money and some responsibility. I'll need business help, because I understand my limitations."

"You want me to help?"

"No," she said quickly. "Not you. Definitely not you.

You need to stop taking care of me, JR. And I need to stop depending on you to take care of me."

"I agree."

"You do?"

"Definitely. You were absolutely right about that."

"Oh. Well, good." She smiled. "But I would be a fool not to take advantage of the fact that between you and Shannon, I could get a recommendation. A referral, you know? To someone you trust? So I can get some sound advice. Get people to handle things I'm not good at, like Barbara said. Part of growing up is knowing what you're good at and what you're not, and when to ask for help."

"A fine insight. Now will you please give me your hands?"

"Excuse me?"

"I want to hold them."

"Oh." She unclasped her hands from around her bent knees and offered them to him.

He held them in his. They were soft and pretty and warm. As was Carmen. "Now, can we get back to what we were talking about a topic or so ago? The part where you tell me you love me?"

"Well, yeah." This time it was a small, shy smile. "I do. I really do. In fact, I can't picture my life without you, JR. I haven't had to, have I? You've always been there. And I want you to keep being there."

"As friends?" he asked with a smile.

She nodded. "Well, sure, as friends. And as lovers, too. Now that I know you *that* way, heck, I'd be a fool to let you go."

"Just lovers?"

"Doesn't that about cover all the bases?"

"Does it?" He was teasing her now, because something tense inside him had just—finally—relaxed completely, and he could afford to.

"Oh, JR. You're really going to make me work for this, aren't you?"

"Yes."

She pouted for a moment, then sighed heavily. "And that's only fair. You've worked so hard for me, haven't you? Wore your heart on your sleeve, even when I pushed you away."

"To the point that I wondered if I would lose you because I couldn't pretend anymore."

"Well, okay, then."

She withdrew her hands from his, got down on her knees and clasped her hands under her chin in a position of supplication. "Stanton Fitzgerald Ewing, JR, will you please marry me and live with me and love me and be the father of my children?"

He sat back and gazed at her. "I'll think about it."

"Oh, you!"

She mock-punched him in the chest. He caught her fists and pulled her onto his lap, where she automatically curled up and rested her head on his shoulder. She'd been doing this for years, forever. The Carmen hug.

"The answer, Goldie Raquel Coyle, aka Carmen, is—" he kissed the top of her head, smelling the sweet, familiar citrus fragrance of her shampoo "—an emphatic, no-holds-barred, unambiguous, most definite, yes."

She sighed. "Whew! Good. I'm so glad your shoulder is better," she said, somewhat out of left field. She raised her head and gazed at him, humor and warmth and, yes, love, shining in her eyes. "JR Two Shoulders, would you please, please kiss me?"

"Glad to oblige," he said, and brought his mouth down to meet hers.

This time he could hug her with both arms. He would have the use of both arms tonight and for all the nights to come.

Finally, he thought. After all these years, he'd been granted the only thing he'd ever really wanted. Carmen in his arms, in his bed, in his life.

Carmen all the time.

* * * * *

Keep reading for an exclusive extract from

High-Stakes Honeymoon
by RaeAnne Thayne,

out in July 2008 from
Mills & Boon® Intrigue.

High-Stakes Honeymoon
by RaeAnne Thayne

Olivia sighed, gazing out at the ripple of waves as she tried to drum up a little enthusiasm for the holiday that stretched ahead of her like the vast, undulating surface of the Pacific. She'd been here less than twenty-four hours and had nine more days to go, and at this point she was just about ready to pack up her suitcases and catch the next puddle jumper she could find back to the States.

She was bored and lonely and just plain miserable.

Maybe she should have invited one of her girlfriends to come along for company. Or better yet, she should have just eaten the cost of the plane tickets and stayed back in Fort Worth.

But then she would have had to face the questions and the sympathetic—and not so sympathetic—looks and the resigned disappointment she was entirely too accustomed to seeing in her father's eyes.

No, this way was better. If nothing else, ten days in another country would give her a little time and distance to handle the bitter betrayal of knowing that even in this, Wallace Lambert wouldn't stand behind her. Her father sided with his golden boy, his groomed successor, and couldn't seem to understand why she might possibly object to her fiancé cheating on her with another woman two weeks before their wedding.

It was apparently entirely unreasonable of her to expect a few basic courtesies—minor little things like fidelity and trust—from the man who claimed to adore her and worship the ground she walked on.

Who knew?

The sun slipped further into the water and she

sighed again, angry at herself. So much for her promise that she wouldn't brood about Bradley or her father.

This was her honeymoon and she planned to enjoy herself, damn them both. She could survive nine more days in paradise, in the company of macaws and howler monkeys, iguanas and even a sloth—not to mention her host, whom she had yet to encounter.

James Rafferty, whom she was meeting later for dinner, had built his fortune through online gambling and he had created an exclusive paradise here completely off the grid—no power except through generators, water from wells on the property. Even her cell phone didn't work here.

Nine days without distractions ought to be long enough for her to figure out what she was going to do with the rest of her life. She was twenty-six years old and it was high time she shoved everybody else out of the driver's seat so she could start picking her own direction.

Some kind of animal screamed suddenly, a high, disconcerting sound, and Olivia jumped, suddenly uneasy to realize she was alone down here on the beach.

There were jaguars in this part of the Osa Peninsula, she had read in the guidebook. Jaguars and pumas and who knew what else. A big cat could suddenly spring out of the jungle and drag her into the trees, and no one in the world would ever know what happened to her.

That would certainly be a fitting end to what had to be the world's worst honeymoon.

She shivered and quickly gathered up her things, shaking the sand out of her towel and tossing her sunglasses and paperback into her beach bag along with her cell phone that she couldn't quite sever herself from, despite its uselessness here.

No worries, she told herself. She seemed to remember jaguars hunted at night and it was still a half hour to full dark. Anyway, she had a hard time believing James Rafferty would allow wild predators such as that to roam free on his vast estate.

Still, she wasn't at all sure she could find her way back to her bungalow in the dark, and she needed to shower off the sand and sunscreen and change for dinner.

She had waited too long to return, she quickly discovered. She would have thought the dying rays of the sun would provide enough light for her to make her way back to her bungalow, fifty yards or so from the beach up a moderate incline. But the trail moved through heavy growth, feathery ferns and flowering shrubs and thick trees with vines roped throughout.

What had seemed lovely and exotic on her way down to the beach suddenly seemed darker, almost menacing, in the dusk.

Something rustled in the thick undergrowth to her left. She swallowed a gasp and picked up her pace, those jaguars prowling through her head again.

Next time she would watch the sunset from the comfort of her own little front porch, she decided nervously. Of course, from what the taciturn housekeeper who had brought her food earlier said, this dry sunset was an anomaly this time of year, given the daily rains.

Wasn't it just like Bradley to book their honeymoon destination without any thought that they were arriving in the worst month of the rainy season. She would probably be stuck in her bungalow the entire nine days.

Still grumbling under her breath, she made it only a few more feet before a dark shape suddenly lurched out of the gathering darkness. She uttered a small shriek of surprise and barely managed to keep her footing.

In the fading light, she could only make out a stranger looming over her, dark and menacing. Something long and lethal gleamed silver in the fading light, and a strangled scream escaped her.

He held a machete, a wickedly sharp one, and she gazed at it, riveted like a bug watching a frog's tongue flicking toward it. She couldn't seem to look away as it gleamed in the last fading rays of the sun.

She was going to die alone on her honeymoon in a foreign country in a bikini that showed just how lousy she was at keeping up with her Pilates.

Her only consolation was that the stranger seemed just as surprised to see her. She supposed someone with rape on his mind probably wouldn't waste time staring at her as if she were some kind of freakish sea creature.

Come on. The bikini wasn't *that* bad.

She opened her mouth to say something—she wasn't quite sure what—but before she could come up with anything, he gave a quick look around, then grabbed her from behind, shoving the hand not holding the machete against her mouth.

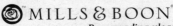

FREE!

4 Books
and a surprise gift!

We would like to take this opportunity to thank you for reading this Mills & Boon® book by offering you the chance to take FOUR more specially selected titles from the Intrigue series absolutely FREE! We're also making this offer to introduce you to the benefits of the Mills & Boon® Reader Service™—

- ★ **FREE home delivery**
- ★ **FREE gifts and competitions**
- ★ **FREE monthly Newsletter**
- ★ **Exclusive Reader Service offers**
- ★ **Books available before they're in the shops**

Accepting these FREE books and gift places you under no obligation to buy. you may cancel at any time. even after receiving your free shipment. Simply complete your details below and return the entire page to the address below. You don't even need a stamp!

YES! Please send me 4 free Intrigue books and a surprise gift. I understand that unless you hear from me. I will receive 6 superb new titles every month for just £3.15 each. postage and packing free. I am under no obligation to purchase any books and may cancel my subscription at any time. The free books and gift will be mine to keep in any case.

18ZEF

Ms/Mrs/Miss/Mr ....Initials ....

BLOCK CAPITALS PLEASE

Surname ....

Address ....

....

....Postcode ....

Send this whole page to:
UK: FREEPOST CN81, Croydon, CR9 3WZ